Stars Don't Cry

CAROLINE AKRILL

Stars Don't Cry

ARMADA

For Em, Especially

First published in the U.K. in 1988 in Armada.

Armada is an imprint of
the Children's Division, part of
the Collins Publishing Group,
8 Grafton Street, London W1X 3LA

Copyright © Caroline Akrill 1988

Printed and bound in Great Britain by
William Collins Sons & Co. Ltd., Glasgow

Contents

1

Cinderella Was Here ...

'Mr Goldstein,' Angel was saying in a strained voice as I arrived at the tackroom door, 'we've got a hearse with one black horse we can let you have tomorrow, but the hearse has shafts, not a pole; you can't just add another horse because you feel like it, not with shafts ... Yes, I'm afraid it's one black horse or nothing, Mr Goldstein ... Yes, two coffins, purple drapes, black plumes or purple ... No, Mr Goldstein, not black *and* purple plumes, black *or* purple ... Well, no of course they won't fall off, they're screwed into a special attachment on top of the bridle; what do you think we do, stick them straight into the horse's head like acupuncture or something?'

Some financial haggling followed which resulted in a figure of two hundred and fifty pounds an hour being agreed for the hire of the hearse with one black horse, plus a flat fee of one hundred pounds for one driver, one pall-bearer and a widow in weeds. 'Yes, Mr Goldstein, I think we can make Pinewood by eleven, I just wish you'd given me proper notice, that's all.' The telephone receiver crashed down. I waited a few seconds before presenting myself in the doorway.

'Excuse me,' I said, 'I'm Grace Vincent.' I used my real name, not my stage name.

Amongst an indescribable jumble of period horse accoutrements; caparisons, armour, plumes, saddlery, and a formidable array of weapons, Angel stood. She looked flushed and cross. She was not very tall, and was slimly built with an extravagant amount of long, dark, curly hair. She was wearing jeans with worn suede chaps on the top, elastic-sided boots, and a cobalt blue shirt which exactly matched the spectacular colour of her eyes. She looked at me in an aggrieved sort of way, as if I had no right to be there, although I had spoken to her by telephone earlier so I knew I was expected.

The strawberry roan with the long white stockings had greeted me with more enthusiasm. Now he stood to attention by my side with his front hooves together. 'The horse met me on the drive,' I volunteered. 'He seems to be loose.'

Angel frowned. 'He seems to be loose,' she said in exactly the same strained tone she had used with Mr Goldstein, 'because he is loose. He's loose because if I shut him in a stable he spends all his time trying to get out and he frets so much that all the flesh drops off him in a week. He's loose because there isn't a fence or a hedge on the place that can contain him.' As if to forestall any further criticism, she added, 'He's loose because he likes to be loose.'

Angel looked with exasperation at the horse who liked to be loose. The strawberry roan dropped his head in a modest sort of way and feigned an interest in the handles of my holdall, nudging them with his velvety nostrils, making gentle blowing noises. Seeing the holdall appeared to remind Angel that, however inconvenient it may be, I had come to stay and something must now be done with me.

'I expect you would like to know where you can dump your things,' she said, 'before you start work.'

'Work?' Despite the fact that I had introduced myself, I wondered if she was still preoccupied with Mr Goldstein and imagined me to be someone else. 'I haven't actually come to work,' I explained, 'I'm here to learn to ride. I'm an actress. I've been sent by A.T.C.' In case she was not familiar with the abbreviation I added, 'By A.T.C. I mean the Ace Television Company.'

'Oh, I know *that*.' Angel tapped the strawberry roan's shoulder with her fingernails and watched with a critical eye as he took a few steps backwards. 'But you won't be able to ride *all* the time, it would be a physical impossibility, wouldn't it? And anyway, if you're not intending to help out, what on earth will you do all day? There isn't much in the way of entertainment on offer in the country, you know. It isn't London, after all. It isn't exactly Soho.'

Did she imagine I thought it would be? I had never met Angel before today, but already I was annoyed by her attitude. I could see I would have to make a stand in order to preserve my rights as a fee-paying customer. 'I'm not expecting to be entertained,' I said firmly. 'When I'm not having lessons, I shall be reading the script for the series. I shall be learning my part.'

Angel frowned.

'A major part in a television serial takes quite a lot of learning,' I pointed out. 'It isn't something you can memorize at the last minute.'

'No,' Angel was forced to concede, 'I don't suppose it is.'

'So I won't have all that much free time to lend a hand,' I told her, 'although I shall be pleased to help out when I can, naturally.'

'Oh,' Angel said. 'Naturally.' She gave me a speculative look. 'You do have the script then?'

It was difficult to know what to say in reply to this because at that moment I had not received it. Yet I saw no advantage in giving Angel an excuse to set me to work in the stables. 'If I didn't have it,' I said, 'I couldn't learn it, could I?'

'No,' Angel agreed, 'you couldn't.' Rather unexpectedly she picked up my holdall. Angel was not a fool. She knew at once the holdall was too light to contain a serial script weighing several pounds, and a single sweeping glance confirmed that I had no other luggage. Triumph flickered momentarily in the cobalt blue eyes. She led the way across the yard with a jaunty step. The strawberry roan watched us go with a benevolent eye.

We skirted a barn whose open doors revealed a motley collection of horse-drawn vehicles. We walked along a row of stables, some of which were occupied, some of which had been swept clean of straw. We circumambulated a muckheap as big as a cottage which radiated steaming clouds of intense fungoid heat.

The stable yard with its pink-washed, peg-tiled buildings had been tidy and well-maintained, but behind the muckheap nature had gained the upper hand. Now Angel led the way along an overgrown path beset on either side by towering nettles, and as she did so her jauntiness faded, her step slowed, her shoulders began to droop. I could see why.

At the end of the path was a long, low farmhouse. The roof was bowed and many of its tiles were missing. The barge-boards and the window-frames were rotten. Plaster had detached itself from the walls in chunks, revealing ancient wattle and daub. It was a depressing sight.

'Look, I may as well warn you that you're going to find the accommodation a bit primitive,' Angel warned as the path became even narrower, the nettles more ominously close. 'We keep promising ourselves we'll do it up – you know, treat the beams, mend the windows, get a new roof, that sort of thing ...'

A gap in the nettles revealed a moat. Its stagnant water was topped with an unwholesome froth of bright green scum and choked with fallen branches. A pair of mallard took fright at our passing and rose into the air, quacking with hysteria.

'The trouble is,' Angel continued, 'there's always something more important to be done first. New fencing to erect, a carriage to be restored; you know how it is.'

By this time we had reached a vast double oak door whose ancient timbers were bleached and cracked by exposure, and whose ornate and mighty hinges were furred with rust. Angel heaved open one of the doors and led the way inside.

Such an entrance hall must once have been fine, with its floor of honey-coloured pammets, its unstained panelling, and its twin fireplaces of arched tudor brick, but it was not so fine today. The plaster ceiling was crumbling and discoloured, and the twin fireplaces overflowed with twigs and soot. There were no carpets on the dirt and straw-strewn floor, there were no curtains at the grime-streaked windows, nor was there a single item of furniture. But Cinderella's coach was there, its interior upholstered in threadbare ivory silk, its exterior stuck all over with yellowing light bulbs, and its dusty silver harness studded with glass diamonds hung from the walls.

'It may not look much when you get this close,' Angel said, 'but from the stalls it's an absolute wow.'

We squeezed past the coach. We walked up a carved and worm-eaten staircase which had never known a sweeping brush to judge by the accumulated dust, chaff and lumps of mud adhering to its treads. At the top the staircase divided itself into two landings, both lit by narrow inadequate windows, both unbelievably gloomy. Angel set off along the landing which led to the left, flipping a light switch in an experimental manner and being rewarded by feeble illumination from the only one of six identical cobwebby wall-lights to be favoured with a bulb.

At the end of the landing Angel dropped my holdall outside a plank door and, after a brief struggle, managed to press down the latch. Because of ancient settlement, the upper floor of the farmhouse sloped at a perilous angle. The door swung inwards of its own accord. What was revealed was less of a bedroom and more of a theatrical costumier's nightmare.

The floorspace was almost totally occupied by clothes-racks, each roughly nailed to the floorboards to halt its inevitable progress down the slope towards the outside wall. Every clothes-rack was bowed by the weight of miscellaneous period clothing. There was no order. Everything looked as though it had been rammed on to its hanger by someone in a demented frenzy. It was chaos. Hunting dress of every era was crammed together with fine Persian battledress; jockey silks in vivid hues, were crushed by the sombre weight of coachmen's many-layered greatcoats; Edwardian side-saddle habits, extravagantly trimmed, were squashed up against the distressed leather, the check and the denim of the cowboy; circus spangles were flattened by military uniforms, and the whole room was pervaded by the unspeakable odour of unwashed clothing, of dust, of musk, and moth.

I am not normally stuck for words. An actress has the mouthings of a host of characters to call upon in extremis, after all, but I could find nothing to say in the face of this. The unexpected eccentricity of the place had taken away my voice. I had not liked the look of the farmhouse from the outside. I had liked it even less from the inside. Now I stood on the threshold of what was to be my room, my refuge, for the next four weeks, and I was appalled.

'I expect you'll feel quite at home amongst the

costumes,' Angel said in a confident tone. 'Actresses are usually born in dressing rooms, aren't they? Cradled in a trunk, or something?'

I wondered if she was slightly deranged. Certainly she was confusing legitimate theatre with life in Variety, when family acts travelled the circuit, and artistes like Vesta Tilley first trod the boards at four years of age. But there was no point in going into all this. 'Now look here, Angel,' I managed to say, 'if you're expecting me to sleep in a trunk, or to roll up for the night in a bundle of old costumes, you can forget it, because I shall ring ATC and make them find me decent accommodation in the village.'

Now it was Angel's turn to be scandalized. 'Decent accommodation in the *village*?' The cobalt eyes regarded me indignantly above a clothes-rack. 'When we've gone to the expense of buying a new *bed*?'

I had not realized there was a bed behind the clothes-racks. But on inspection, hedged in on three sides by dusty costumes, there was a new-looking single divan, complete with duvet and a cheerful buttercup yellow cover. Somehow the knowledge that whoever 'we' comprised had spent money on a bed expressly for my comfort, when there were horses to feed, fences to erect and carriages to restore, softened my heart. I was grateful. 'Oh, really,' I protested, 'you shouldn't have bothered.'

'Well I know we shouldn't have *bothered*.' Angel bounced my holdall on to the duvet in an impatient manner. 'I did *tell* Anthony it was a waste of money. I *said* you would be just as happy on the camp bed, but he wouldn't listen, he bought it all the same.' Her face assumed a browbeaten expression. 'Well, you know what Anthony's *like*,' she said in a despondent tone, 'you can't tell him anything.'

As I had no idea what Anthony was like, having not as yet been introduced, I could neither agree nor disagree with this criticism of his character, but I was vastly heartened to think I had such a powerful ally. With a bed I would dare to sleep in and a friend like generous, strong-minded Anthony, I thought I might just manage to survive four weeks of Angel and the incredibly awful farmhouse.

It was not that I had expected luxury, far from it. I had known that whatever accommodation was offered would be spartan. I had even been prepared to share a room with another girl, or be bunked in a dormitory like a boarding school. But I had expected to arrive at an equitation centre; a briskly efficient, purposeful place, with acres of grazing enclosed by immaculate white-painted post and rail fencing, with covered schools and paddocks of show jumps striped in bright, primary colours. What I had expected was an educational establishment, a place of learning, full of other students, staffed by trained instructors with strings of qualifications as proof of their ability. The peeling sign at the end of the lumpy drive had been the first indication that this was not to be the case. MOAT FARM STABLES, it had read. HORSES AND EQUIPAGES SUPPLIED FOR FILM AND TELEVISION WORK.

In a way perhaps I should have been pleased by this, even relieved. I was an actress after all, and to me a professional riding establishment, hair-netted, BHS approved, would have been an alien place. Moat Farm sounded closer to my world. Why, it was almost show-business. But somehow I had not been pleased. I had felt uneasy. I had been suspicious. Eleven months looking for work under the wing of an unlicensed agent who worked from a corner booth of a Soho café had taught me many things, amongst them that nobody was to be trusted in

14

the world of stage and screen, and that nothing could be counted on, nothing was binding, not even a contract signed by both parties on the bottom line. Forty-nine weeks in the dole queue and over thirty unsuccessful auditions had shown me that if anything could go wrong, it would go wrong. I had been made wary.

Standing at the foot of the drive, staring at the sign, I had begun to feel the first prickling of doubt about the television company who had sent me to Moat Farm. I wondered why. I wondered if for some reason they considered me unworthy of a proper training establishment, or if they were under-financed and would gradually reveal themselves as insolvent and cheeseparing; if this was an example of how things were going to be achieved – on a low budget, at cut-price, on the cheap.

Angel was now wandering up and down the floorboards, poking at the clothes-racks in a desultory manner. 'These costumes need a good brush,' she decided, 'they ought to be put into bags, but think of the time it would take.'

I sat on the buttercup yellow duvet, wishing she would leave.

'If I left you a brush, I don't suppose – in your spare time …?'

'I won't have any spare time,' I said.

'Does anyone have any spare time these days?' Angel wondered. 'I know I don't. There's always far too much work to be done and never enough hours in the day, and it's Anthony's *fault*. He won't have anyone unskilled about the place, and he won't *hear* of getting cheap labour on the pretext of training youngsters for examinations like the riding schools do.'

'Good for Anthony,' I said. And if you imagine you are going to use me as cheap labour for the next few weeks, I thought, you can think again.

'As for properly trained people,' Angel continued, 'they ask for the most *colossal* wages, and they can get more than we can afford to pay on the dole these days.'

I knew all about the dole. I also knew how much Mr Goldstein was paying for the hire of the hearse with one black horse, a driver, a pall-bearer, and a widow in weeds. So I was not prepared to offer sympathy to Angel as she pleaded penury.

'If you wouldn't mind,' I said impatiently, 'I need to unpack and change into something suitable for riding. I can find my own way back to the yard.'

'Are you expecting a lesson this afternoon?' Angel gave me a foxy look. 'I thought you had something *far* more important to do.'

'Such as what?'

'Such as learning the script you haven't got.'

I thought her jodhpur boots made a quite unnecessary din as she rattled triumphantly down the staircase.

2

It's Supposed to be a Sport

The landing window opposite the plank door opened easily, but the one in the room with the clothes-racks and the bed was stuck fast to its frame, despite its rotted appearance. From a pile of equestrian accessories heaped up anyhow in a corner, I extracted a heavy brass stirrup, shaped like a slipper with a pointed toe. I was quite prepared to use it as a battering ram, but the little window surrendered at the first assault, jumping open as if in fright, letting in the cool afternoon air and creating enough of a through draught to blow away the musty smell.

I was in no hurry to make my way back to the stable yard where Angel might, or might not, be waiting to give me my first lesson. Yet there seemed no point in unpacking my holdall, because there was no wardrobe, no chest of drawers, and no room on the clothes-racks for anything of mine.

I changed my pink cotton overalls for jeans, a jersey and rubber riding boots. Along the landing in an antiquated bathroom where one wall was completely taken up by an ornate gilt-framed mirror, its glass patterned with ugly, bruise-like marks, and where the windowsill was heaped with dead bluebottles, I washed hastily in tepid water coaxed from a brass tap afflicted with verdigris, and tidied and plaited my hair.

My hair had helped to win me the part; at least, it had made Tom Sylvester notice me, because at the audition he had asked if I was wearing a hairpiece.

I had not known he was Tom Sylvester then, of course.

He just appeared to be a rather rude young man with dark hair and brooding eyes who sat slumped into a plastic chair beside the Casting Director, with his chin sunk into the upturned collar of his anorak and his eyes closed.

He had opened one eye when he enquired if I was wearing a hairpiece and I, the last the be seen at the end of an interminable and seemingly fruitless audition, and thinking it all a complete waste of time, had snapped that my hair was my own.

I might have been more polite had I known to whom I was speaking, but how could I have known? Writers are not like actors, after all. One can often recognize an actor by his face, even if one cannot quite recall his name, but writers are the faceless people. Even their names only become familiar if they are phenomenally successful – like Tom Sylvester, for example. When a Tom Sylvester serial was shown on television practically everyone in the country stopped what they were doing and watched.

Yet at the audition there he sat, Tom Sylvester in person, squinting at me with one eye and demanding to know if I was wearing a hairpiece. When I snapped out my reply he said, 'OK, keep your hair on, Grace Darling.'

I had scowled at the joke, not finding it amusing, but he had given me the part, the female lead in his serial, without asking to hear any of my prepared pieces, without having heard me read from any script, just like that.

Even now, it still seemed incredible that it could have happened that way. At the time I was so dumbfounded, I did not really believe it could be true. I believed it even less when the Casting Director told me they had seen over two hundred girls before me, and Tom Sylvester had not addressed a word to one of them. '... not a flicker of an eyelid until you came along,' the Casting Director told me, 'and normally I'd have a short-listed dozen by now. So let's forget he didn't hear you read, because you've got yourself the part, Grace Darling, and you've got Equity as from this minute – you can ride?' he added.

Across the dusty floor of the audition hall I looked at him and my heart skidded into my ribs. 'Ride?' I said.

'Ride,' the Casting Director said heavily. 'You've heard of horseback riding? It's supposed to be a sport – you wear a skid-lid to protect your brain, and you sit between the ears and the tail.' As the implication of my obvious bewilderment hit him, he stared at me, appalled. 'You must be able to ride, Grace Darling! This is a television serial about a horse we're casting for! Jesus Christ Superstar, it was *the* audition requirement, it's top priority, we did *say*!'

But nobody had said anything to me. Especially not my agent, Ziggy Stanislavski of Starlight Promotions, who had only sent me along to audition as a long-shot when he had heard by means of the Soho grapevine that the project was in danger of being shelved because Tom Sylvester couldn't find his female lead.

And so, desperate to find work after months of the dole queue and thirty unsuccessful auditions, I had lied in order to keep the part. I assured the Casting Director that I could ride when I had never sat on a horse in my life, and I prayed that I would have time to learn before anyone found out. But I was foiled at the location film test when, without any warning, the Director produced a horse for me to ride ...

I closed the door on the hideous little bathroom and made my way down the staircase. Cinderella's dusty pumpkin coach hardly looked substantial enough to carry a flesh and blood princess. Close inspection revealed that it was not expected to because there was no floor in it. Cinderella had to walk. This was typical of the theatrical profession, but also rather depressing. The coach that looked a wow from the stalls was revealed as a sham when one drew near, in the same way that the pieces of eight that glittered in the spotlights would be revealed as bottle tops that tore the actor's fingers.

Not that I was unaware that the whole art of acting was based upon pretence, on the peddling of illusions and the faking of emotions, however sincerely and honestly performed.

Ziggy had not failed to remind me how it was many times. 'You're in the business of deception now, Kiddo, and don't you forget it. You got to make the punters identify with people who don't exist, you got to make them believe things that aren't true, you got to make them see things that aren't there, and if you don't feel up to it, Grace Darling, if you got any doubts, then you better go find a typing school instead, because there's no way you're gonna get out from the wings.'

Well, I was almost out from the wings, but not because I had managed to deceive anyone about my prowess on horseback at the location film test. I had not managed to fool anyone for long . . .

I had gaped at the horse in shock and total despair, knowing that in front of everyone, Director and film crew, I was about to be exposed as a liar and a cheat, and that nothing I could say or do could avert it.

Only one thing enabled me to find the courage to get into the saddle, and that was my hatred for the handler of the horse, a dark, restless and bad-tempered individual who had guessed as soon as he saw me that I had lied about my riding ability, and who wasted no time in telling me he did not allow his horses to be messed about by novices, and that if I damaged his precious animal I would surely answer for the consequences. His scorn and hostility spurred me to carry on, to try and bluff my way through the test, but of course, it had been a vain hope.

I lost control almost at once and was the cause of an accident when the horse tried to jump a cyclist who had unexpectedly appeared in his path. The tracking vehicle collided with a lamp-post, and at the exact moment that I hit the ground, many thousand pounds worth of Arriflex camera was precipitated on to the pavement.

The handler was first on the scene, but he raced past me, leaving me lying where I had landed, not caring if I was alive or dead, shouting that I was a stupid, empty-headed little fool, had I any idea how much the horse was worth; as if in comparison my life, my injuries, counted for nothing; as if next to the horse, I was of no account.

During the ensuing confusion I had crept away, certain that I had lost the part, shocked, humiliated, and in tears. But I had reckoned without the uncertainty of the acting profession, and the fact that uncertainty can work both ways. At any audition you can be confident you have given an impressive performance yet fail to please, or you can feel positive you have failed most miserably in your presentation, and land the part. I had landed the part. In spite of lying to the Casting Director, in spite of invoking vitriolic wrath in the handler of the horse, in spite of causing thousands of pounds worth of damage to the camera, and wrecking the cyclist's new machine, I had landed the part, and that was all that mattered. A chance to show what I could do was all I had dreamed of, and now I had that chance.

Standing beside the pumpkin coach in which Cinderella must walk to the Ball, I reminded myself that in just over four weeks' time I would be playing the female lead in a Tom Sylvester television serial, a part which would make me instantly recognizable to at least half of the population of the country, a part which would set me on the road to stardom. Such knowledge was as heartening as it was unbelievable. Such knowledge would help me through the next four weeks in this unnervingly eccentric place. Such knowledge would jolly well have to.

I pushed open one of the massive, weathered doors and stepped out into the sunshine, breathing in the fragrant, heady air of the countryside, looking across what once had been a garden but was now a wilderness in which even the roses had reverted to their natural state, to the dark, deep woods beyond. Naturally, gardening would not be a priority at Moat Farm. In my imagination I heard Angel say, 'If I found you a spade, I don't suppose – in your spare time …?'

In a resigned, but slightly more optimistic frame of mind I walked back towards the yard along the narrow path between the towering nettles, wondering what Angel would be like as a riding instructress.

But Angel was no longer in the tack room. Neither was she to be found in the barn. Nor was she in any of the loose boxes I peered into, although many of the equine occupants hurried to their doors at my approach, some to greet me in a friendly manner, some to threaten by laying back their ears and making menacing faces.

It was in the last stable of all that I found someone. It was not Angel. But it was someone I knew. Someone I recognized.

In the act of flinging a rug over the very same black horse I had ridden at the location film test, turning to the door at the sound of my footsteps, watching without surprise but with unmistakable satisfaction as the expression on my face changed from stark incredulity to horrified stupefaction, was the handler.

3

They Shoot Horses Do They?

'Well,' Anthony said in a malevolent voice, 'if it isn't our empty-headed little actress friend, Grace Darling.'

Through the open doorway, over the straw bedding which separated us, I stared at him, mesmerized as a rabbit caught in the headlamps of a car. 'You?' I said weakly. 'Oh no, not you ... it *can't* be.'

'But why not?' The thin, well-shaped lips were smiling, but the eyes were as hostile as ever. 'Why shouldn't it be me?'

I made no reply. Had I given the matter any consideration at all I might have guessed, but I had not given it a moment's thought. I had been far too occupied with the unpromising nature of my reception and with the hideousness of the farmhouse to wonder who 'we' comprised; to ponder the identity of Anthony, of whom Angel had said in her brow-beaten way '... you know what he's *like*, you can't tell him anything.' Now I gazed at him mutely; rendered entirely speechless by the twist of fate that had delivered me into his stable yard; astounded that he, of all people, should turn out to be Anthony.

'Of course, I can give you several reasons why it *should* be me,' Anthony said, leaning against the black horse's shoulder in a deliberately casual manner, hooking his thumbs through the belt-loops of his breeches. 'First, because I happen to specialize in teaching actors and actresses the rudiments of horsemanship to ascertain that they do not ruin every horse they come into contact with ...'

23

I should have realized. Why had I not guessed? I leaned back against the door-frame for support.

'... second, because I am the owner of the horse you will be riding in the serial, which gives me a vested interest in your progress ...'

I might have known it. It was obvious that the horse they used for the location film test would also appear in the film. Why, the Director had even told me so himself. When I had protested that I was unprepared for riding and had demanded that the co-star should ride instead, the Director had looked at me in amazement. 'What d'you mean, let the co-star do it?' he had said. 'The *horse* is the co-star!'

'... furthermore, I have been appointed Horsemaster for the filming of *The Hooves of the Horses* which, in case you had forgotten, is the title of the serial you are supposedly the star of. And finally,' said Anthony, 'because I think you need to be taught a lesson about horses you won't forget in a hurry, Grace Darling, and I am *just* the person to make damned sure you learn it.'

The man was insufferable. Shaken as I was, I felt a resurgence of loathing for him; for his unspeakable arrogance, for the contemptuous way he had said 'in case you had forgotten' and 'supposedly the star of'. Stunned as I was, I could not let him get away with it. I took a deep breath. I found my voice. 'I think you should explain precisely what you mean by a lesson I won't forget in a hurry,' I said angrily. 'ATC have sent me here to learn to ride, not to give you the opportunity to settle an imaginary score.'

'Imaginary?' The dark eyes narrowed. 'I doubt very much if any score I have to settle would be imaginary, Grace Darling, but if you really want me to explain what I mean then I shall be happy to oblige.' He smiled again, a thin, humourless smile, and ran a caressing hand down the black horse's neck. 'You, in common with a great many members of your so-called profession, are a selfish, egotistical little bitch, and if you are going to work with my horses you have to change your attitude ...'

This was altogether too much. 'Now wait a minute,' I interrupted furiously, 'I don't have to stand here and listen to this!' Nor did I intend to do so. I turned to leave but Anthony was at the door in an instant and his fingers had locked above my elbow like a clamp. I tried, but it was impossible to pull away.

'You *do* have to listen, Grace Darling.' The dark and dangerous face was uncomfortably close to mine. I was not going to allow myself to be intimidated, but all the same my heart began to thud in an uncomfortable manner and my throat dried. 'I shall make you hear me, even if I am obliged to fit hobbles to your ankles and a halter round your neck in order to restrain you.' The voice was menacingly soft, the eyes like flint. 'You didn't care about anything at the film test apart from your own chances, did you? The only thing that mattered was how good you looked for the camera. The only thing *you* cared about was cheating your way into a part which you were not entitled to ...'

I did not want to hear this. I did not want to look at him. I twisted my face away.

'... the fact that you had no idea how to ride, knew nothing about horses, that you had lied your way into the test, the fact that *your* ignorance put *my* horse at risk, endangering its life, didn't matter to you, did it?'

I was not going to answer him. I had nothing to say. I saw no point in entering into argument because as soon as he released me I was going to leave. I was not going to stay at Moat Farm – not for ATC, not for Tom Sylvester, not for anyone or anything – not with Anthony in charge.

'*Did* it?'

A hand of steel took hold of my chin, turned my unwilling head. I had been determined not to speak, but now I was forced to say something in my own defence. 'I *didn't* endanger the horse's life!' I burst out. 'How can you say that? How *dare* you make accusations against me when they are totally untrue! I didn't hurt your horse at all!' In order to exonerate myself I tried to remember exactly what had happened, whether I had been guilty of negligence as well as ignorance, but I could only recall the shock of the horse's sudden appearance on the scene, and the feeling of numbing despair as the Director had steered me purposefully towards the empty saddle. I could remember thinking how beautiful he was, the black horse, the perpetuator of my downfall; how his coat had gleamed like satin; how the long mane had been slippery as silk when I touched it; but had I really considered for one moment that the horse might be damaged as a consequence of my inexperience? The unwelcome truth of the matter was that I had not, and the realization did not help my current predicament one little bit.

'All right, so I *didn't* consider the horse! I know it sounds naive, but it looked big enough and strong enough to take care of itself ... I thought ... I *knew*, if anyone was going to be hurt it would be *me*!'

I looked directly into the dark and angry eyes as I spoke so that even Anthony, who couldn't be told anything, would realize that it was the truth. Abruptly I felt myself released. Now it was Anthony who turned aside, moving back to the black horse. 'But it wasn't you who was hurt, was it, Grace Darling?' he said bitterly. 'You escaped with a few bruises. It was The Raven who was lamed for five weeks. It was The Raven who, but for the intervention of the Almighty, might have been permanently damaged!'

The Raven lame for five weeks? He could not have been! I could not believe it. I stared at Anthony. I stared at The Raven, at his strong-looking, whole-looking, gleaming legs, at his beautiful face and the way his pricked ears followed our argument, flicking from one to the other, his generously deep and liquid eyes overlaid with anxiety at the displeasure in his master's voice.

'But I didn't know! I honestly had no idea!'

'Of course you had no idea.' Anthony picked up a leather roller from the corner of the stable, placing it behind The Raven's well-defined withers in order to secure the blanket, reaching easily under the horse's belly for the straps. 'It wouldn't have occurred to *you* to enquire. But why should you care? It wouldn't have mattered to you if The Raven had broken a bone and been shot as a result of it, as long as you got the part you wanted.'

He was determined to show me no mercy. But of course, in his eyes I did not deserve any. 'You've no right to say that,' I said, 'it isn't fair. And it isn't true either. Horses don't *always* have to be shot if they break a bone – what about Mill Reef?'

Anthony looked round at me, obviously surprised that I should even remember the horse's name. 'Mill Reef was a successful racehorse and a stallion who could earn his owners millions in stud fees,' he said in a cold voice. 'The Raven has been gelded. His useful life would have been over. If what happened to Mill Reef had happened to The Raven there would have been no second career open to him. He would have had a bullet put through his brain.'

'Don't!' Involuntarily I glanced at The Raven's head, at the wide brow under the long, silken forelock, and my stomach jumped at the thought of it. 'How can you even *say* it!'

'I can say it because I want you to know how it is with

horses, Grace Darling, because it's important. It's part of your education.' Anthony turned, slipping a protective arm across the horse's neck. The Raven turned his head and touched him gently with his nose. I was not sure if horses knew about love, but it seemed that The Raven loved Anthony. And if his horses loved him, who knew him best, then surely he could not be as hateful as he appeared.

'They don't put plaster casts on horses' legs, because we can't actually speak their language, we can't explain. Horses don't understand – they try to escape from them, they panic, they throw themselves about and cause even more damage. And so they are shot.' Anthony gave me one of his humourless smiles. '*They Shoot Horses Don't They*. To you, it's just a film title; to me, it's a fact of life.'

How could it be? Was he just exaggerating in order to punish me? After all, if horses were such fragile creatures, if every move we made, every scene we shot, was to be benighted by the ever-present, terrifying possibility of broken bones and bullets through the brain, how on earth would we ever film the series?

'Of course,' Anthony went on in a level voice, 'you are not the first actress to damage a horse just for the sake of the camera, far from it. Horses have always been looked upon as expendable in your profession. The actors and stuntsmen in the Westerns were probably the worst offenders. They used trip wires to make sure the horses fell in the right places. Six times out of ten the poor devils broke their necks.'

I stared at him in disbelief. Could it be true? Yet why would he lie? Would I ever be able to watch a Western again without being agonized by every fall? Without wondering if the horse would scramble to its feet when the camera had moved on, or simply continue to lie there …

'Historical Drama was almost as bad. Coach horses were blinkered or blindfolded to be driven over cliffs just to get the shots. Horses were even shipwrecked, thrown overboard, dropped into the sea with no hope of recovery, drowned, just for the camera ...'

'Stop it!' No wonder he was so fiercely protective about his horses. These things were barbaric, horrific ...

'Then there were the epics. Remember *Ben Hur*? A hundred and fifty horses were killed just filming the chariot racing scenes – remember that when you next watch it.'

'As if I could – knowing *that*!' I turned to the doorway, sickened. For the first time in my life I was ashamed of my chosen profession. How could people have justified such atrocities? Who had allowed such monstrous cruelties to be perpetuated in the name of entertainment? This time Anthony allowed me to leave.

I blundered into Angel, carrying a coiled lunge and a whip. 'Oh, there you are,' she said in an annoyed tone. 'I've been looking for you *everywhere*.'

'Angel,' I said weakly, as we walked along the row of stables, 'when Anthony supplied the horse for the location film test, after I'd made such a mess of it, did anyone contact him afterwards? Was he consulted? Did anyone ask for his opinion?'

'There was a telephone call, if that's what you mean. And I know he said he would be glad to have the opportunity to turn you into a rider, because I was listening. He actually said he couldn't wait.'

'I bet he couldn't,' I said with feeling.

4

Remember Ben Hur?

'Richard?' I had found a telephone. I needed to talk to someone.

'Grace. This *is* a surprise.'

The sarcastic tone dashed all hope of comfort. 'You might sound a little more welcoming.'

'Welcoming?' There was a chilly pause. 'Grace, I feel sure I don't need to remind you of what you said to me the night you left.'

'No,' I agreed, 'you don't. I know what I said, but ...'

'A separation, you wanted. A cooling-off period. We were getting too heavily involved. I won't contact you, you said, and you must promise not to contact me. Your words, Grace, not mine. Your decision.'

'Richard listen, I know I said that, but ...'

'It isn't as if it's the first time, Grace. It's happened before. It's happened too many times. To be perfectly honest, I'm getting tired of it. I'm asking myself if it's worth it.'

This was well-worn territory.

'I appreciate you have to consider your career ...'

'I *do* have to consider my career. It's important that I make a success of it, Richard. You *know* that.'

'I realize that this is your big chance ...'

'The serial *is* my big chance, it could be my *only* chance. If I make a mess of this, if I fluff it ...'

'I know this isn't a good time to become deeply involved ...'

'It isn't because I don't want to, it's because I can't

afford to be involved. All my energies have to be put into my work ...'

'All your emotions ...'

'All my emotions need to be directed towards ... Richard, you are *mocking* me!'

'The whole affair is a mockery, Grace! All I'm demonstrating is that I know the responses off by heart. I've heard them so many times. As a matter of fact I am sick and tired of hearing them!'

I closed my eyes. I must have been out of my mind to ring Richard when we had parted on such difficult terms. 'Are you telling me you don't want to see me again?'

'I didn't actually say that.'

'No, but ...'

'You used me, Grace. You used me for six weeks. You encouraged me to believe that things were working out, then off you went to pursue your career and told me not to try to contact you. Where did that leave me? How was I supposed to feel?'

'I didn't *use* you; that's an *awful* thing to say ...'

'You used me, Grace. It's perfectly true, and you know it. After six weeks together you cut me off without a word. No wonder I'm not welcoming,' Richard said.

It seemed I had some explaining to do. 'It wasn't an easy decision,' I pointed out. 'It wasn't done lightly, but it did seem the fairest thing to do. I only did what I thought best.'

'Best for whom?' Richard enquired. 'It certainly wasn't best for me.'

'Nor for me,' I admitted. 'That's why I'm ringing. I was wrong to say we shouldn't stay in touch. I miss you.'

There was a silence. Eventually Richard said 'Oh yes?' His voice was sceptical.

'I *have* made the first move, you must allow me that.'

Another silence. 'I suppose I must,' he said grudgingly.

31

'Richard, what I said may have seemed unfair, and I *was* being selfish in a way, I *was* thinking about my career, I won't deny that ...'

'How very magnanimous of you to admit it!'

'... but I was also thinking of you! Of how unreasonable it would be to expect you to wait round whilst I was away for months at a time ...'

'I have never waited around exactly,' Richard said.

'... and how unfair it would be to expect you to be faithful...'

'I've *never* been faithful.'

'I know!' I cried. 'So what would be the use of expecting it! What would be the point!'

'The point is that we have always had an unspoken agreement,' Richard said in a calm voice. 'If you choose to go off and pursue an acting career I can't stop you, but at least you know I'm here, so why stay out of contact? What point is there in that?'

'There doesn't seem to be any point.'

'So you have changed your mind, and now you are ringing to apologize?'

'Yes.'

'I see.'

'Is that all you have to say?'

'I'm waiting for you to apologize.'

'I'm sorry,' I said wearily.

'And you think that makes everything all right?'

I sighed. 'I don't know what to think. I don't know what you expect.'

'I expect too much, Grace. I thought you knew that – you have told me often enough – but I also expect you have another motive for ringing me.'

'Another motive? What other motive could I possibly have?'

'I expect you are miserable,' Richard said in a smug

voice. 'I expect the riding school does not live up to your expectations. I expect you don't like it, Grace, and I further expect that far from ringing me to apologize, you rang me for support, for sympathy!'

'Sympathy! From *you*!' It was laughable. 'Why, you haven't an ounce of sympathy in your body! You are the *last* person I would ring for sympathy!'

'Not quite the last. Who else could you appeal to? Not your long-suffering mother, because she has never approved of your trying to be an actress ...'

I had underestimated Richard. He knew me too well.

'... nor would you ring your decidedly dodgy agent, because he stands to lose his miserable ten per cent if you opt out ...'

'How dare you accuse Ziggy of being dodgy!'

'Oh, so there *is* something going on betweeen you two after all! I've often wondered!'

'Don't judge everyone by your own standards of fidelity!'

'Well, Grace Darling.' Now that he had managed to turn the tables, Richard's voice sounded amused. '*Are* you miserable?'

How could I possibly admit it now? 'Of course I'm not miserable. As a matter of fact, I've just had my first riding lesson.'

'So now you're an expert.'

'Hardly. I spent half an hour circling round on a lunge rein with no reins and stirrups, doing suppling exercises. The horse didn't even go out of a walk.'

'Did you enjoy it?'

'I did, actually.' This was not the untruth it might have been. I might easily have enjoyed it had I not still been haunted by images of the equine carnage wreaked by the chariot racing scenes in *Ben Hur*.

'What's the accommodation like?'

33

I thought of the accommodation; of the hideous farmhouse with its bulging walls and falling plaster. I thought of my room with its sloping floor and musty costumes. I thought of the beastly little bathroom with its luke-warm water and its sills heaped with dead blue-bottles. 'The accommodation's fine,' I said. 'It isn't splendid, but it's quite adequate. My bed is new.'

'Food?'

'I haven't had any yet.' Nor was I certain that any would be offered. In the brick-floored kitchen next to the untidy office where I had located the telephone, there was nothing remotely evocative of food. The Aga was cold and covered with a layer of dust. There was an electric kettle on an old pine dresser empty of plates, a jar of cheap instant coffee, a packet of white sugar. I had pulled open the refrigerator and seen two bottles of milk, half a packet of bright yellow margarine, and two sausages with an unhealthy pink bloom on their skins.

'What about the people?'

'The people are charming,' I said firmly. I was tired of Richard's investigations and determined to give nothing away.

'In that case I shall drive over to see you,' he decided.

'*What*?'

'I said I would drive over to see you. You needn't sound so astonished. You made the first move. I shall make the second.'

'But Richard, I'm not sure that I ... I mean, I don't know if ...'

'You do want to see me again, Grace?'

'Well,' I said, flustered. 'I ...'

'You told me you missed me. That you were wrong to say we shouldn't stay in touch. You said it only a few minutes ago.'

'I know, but ...'

'I can't come this week because all my appointments are arranged, so it will have to be next week. It might even be the week after that, but I shall come. I'll ring first.' Richard was Deputy Managing Director of his father's company. He had a proper job.

I gave him the telephone number, reading from the grubby dial of the old-fashioned black telephone. I told myself at least I had time to think up some ploy to put him off, to prevent his arrival. Somehow I would be able to stop him coming to Moat Farm.

'That will be lovely,' I told him, 'I shall look forward to it.'

'Me too.' He was about to say something more, but his attention was diverted by the urgent shrilling of another telephone. Richard's father and mine had been firm friends from childhood. That I should marry Richard, settle down in my home village of Wallingford and forget all about acting was my mother's dearest wish.

I put down the telephone receiver. Angel was sitting on the kitchen table, swinging her legs. As there was no connecting door, she had obviously been listening to every word. The cobalt eyes were speculative and also vaguely anxious. 'Boyfriend?' she wanted to know.

I nodded briefly. I was not about to embark upon a discussion of my most private affairs with Angel.

'Is he good-looking?'

I thought of Richard's smoothly handsome face, his natural and somewhat infuriating elegance, and the way his fair hair fell into his beautiful blue eyes fringed with thick lashes. 'No,' I said, 'he's rather ugly actually.'

Angel shrugged. 'Looks aren't everything though, are they? Are you in love with him?'

Her curiosity was boundless. 'Certainly not. If you must know, not only is he ugly, he's also conceited and totally insensitive, and I just wish he would stop pestering me.' None of this was true, but it seemed to satisfy Angel.

'Good,' she said. 'It makes things easier if you're unattached. You will pay for the call?' she added cheerfully as I made my escape. 'Long-distance before six costs a bomb these days.'

Climbing the wormy stairs, feeling the top of my thighs stiffening after my lunge-lesson, I wondered what had put her in such a good humour. Then I remembered my description of the farmhouse and its occupants and decided it was probably the first time in her life that Angel had heard herself and Anthony described as charming.

5

You'll just be a Black Widow

Sustenance came from an unexpected source. The evening meal arrived in a van, delivered by one of the catering staff from the local hostelry, The Hare and Hounds.

'I never cook,' Angel said, throwing cutlery around the scarred kitchen table, plopping down petrol station tumblers, and filling a plastic jug with water from the tap. 'I don't have the time. I mean, if you cook, you also have to shop. How could I possibly fit it all in? How would I cope?' She flopped down into a chair and stared at her meal – boiled-in-the-bag Coq au Vin, overcooked frozen peas, and a generous portion of limp french fries – in a circumspect manner.

'That isn't exactly true.' Anthony, who had been sitting at the table for some time, put aside his copy of *Horse and Hound*. 'Angel used to cook, but then there was the little episode of the casserole.'

'The casserole?'

'I made a casserole,' Angel explained, 'a large one. I thought it would last a few days. Then we were called out to do some filming because Hender Copper's faller went lame ...'

'Hender Copper's faller?'

'Hender Copper could be regarded as the enemy,' Anthony said in a grim tone. 'He's the opposition. And a faller is a horse trained to fall *without* trip wires.'

'I see,' I said hastily. 'Quite.' I hoped he would not ask me to remember *Ben Hur*, not just as I was about to begin my supper. As the others were already eating, I picked up my fork and speared a chip in a half-hearted manner. I was tired. All my bones ached from the lunge lesson, and I had spent the latter part of the afternoon scrubbing out water buckets.

'All the buckets need cleaning out,' Angel had sighed. 'If I found you a scrubbing brush, I don't suppose you could ...?' Well, there had been little else to occupy my time.

'Anyway,' Angel continued, 'we were away for three days and when we got back it was late at night and we were absolutely starving. So I warmed up the casserole.'

'But not too much,' Anthony added, 'only enough to wake up the Salmonella bacteria.'

'The results were rather dire,' Angel admitted.

'Yes, I expect they were.' I looked unhappily at my plate. The Coq au Vin glowed with an unwholesome brilliance which owed more to cochineal than to vin. The french fries sprawled in the watery sauce, luke-warm, flaccid and glistening. I have never liked frozen peas.

'Still,' Angel said, brightening, 'as we shall be filming tomorrow, I expect we shall be quite decently fed.'

'We?' I remembered Mr Goldstein.

'We would hardly leave you behind. It wouldn't be fair, would it? So we've included you in our plans. You can come with us.' Angel then countered this philanthropic speech by adding, 'As a matter of fact we need another person, so you will be doing us a favour really.'

I put down my fork. 'I don't do favours,' I said.

Both Anthony and Angel stopped eating. They stared at me.

'What did you say?' Anthony's face stiffened.

'I said I don't do favours. That isn't what I'm here for. ATC sent me here to learn to ride, and if you two are going filming, what happens about *my* riding lesson?'

Clearly this was not the response Angel was expecting. She frowned.

'There won't be a riding lesson, that's what happens,' Anthony said. 'Riding lessons take second place when there is filming to be done. Filming is our livelihood.'

'And acting is mine,' I snapped. 'That's why I'm here. Not to perform favours for you, but to have riding lessons.'

'You will *get* your lessons,' Angel said in a reassuring tone. 'It isn't as if we are trying to cheat you out of them. I shall give you extra time afterwards to make up. And as we have to go tomorrow in any case, you may as well come along. Otherwise what will you do all day?'

'I shall learn my part.'

The cobalt eyes narrowed. 'You haven't got a script.'

'It will probably arrive in tomorrow's post.'

'It won't.'

I glared. 'How do you know it won't?'

Angel dropped her eyes to her plate. 'I just wouldn't expect it to arrive that soon, that's all. ATC are sure to give you time to settle in,' she said in a careful voice.

As if I should ever settle in! As if I wanted to! I stared at her in exasperation. 'I expect I shall find some way to occupy my time,' I said crossly, 'even if I'm reduced to mucking out the stables.'

'A quaint idea, but not possible, I'm afraid,' Anthony said in a cold voice. 'You will have to come with us. You have no choice.'

Did he imagine that left alone in the stable yard I would run amok amongst the horses – fix up a few trip wires perhaps or stage chariot races to break their legs? 'What do you mean, I have no choice?' I demanded.

'I mean that I shall take you by force if you won't come willingly.'

He couldn't be serious. I looked at his face and decided he was perfectly serious. 'You can't do that!'

'You think I can't?' Anthony leaned back in his chair

39

and surveyed me with steely amusement. 'As I said before, it's part of your education Grace Darling, and lesson number one is that learning about horses isn't just about sitting on top, looking like a rider, it's about familiarization. It's about handling horses, getting a feel for them, getting to know how they react to things; it's about trying to understand how their minds work.'

'I know all about that!' I was not going to listen to another lecture, 'But ...'

'You don't know!' Anthony said sharply. 'That's just your problem! You imagine you know a lot of things, but actually you know nothing!'

Of course he was prejudiced. Because of what happened at the film test he had formed a completely false opinion of me and nothing I could say would change his mind, but I was not going to allow him to infer that I was an idiot. 'I'm used to people assuming that I'm stupid,' I flared. 'I've managed to come to terms with the fact that most people assume that any actress not plain enough to be classified as serious, is just a decorative nitwit, but I am *not* prepared ...'

'If you are trying to tell me you have a *brain*,' Anthony interrupted in a malicious tone, 'then I suggest you use it. I am in charge of your training schedule, and if I say a day or two with the horses spent filming is part of that schedule, there is not a lot you can do about it.'

'I don't need to do a *lot*,' I said. 'All I need to do is complain to ATC.'

If I had imagined that this would trounce Anthony, I was mistaken. He gave me one of his thin smiles.

'You could,' he agreed, 'but then so could I. And I could tell them how uncooperative you are, and how inept you appear in the saddle. I could explain to ATC that due to physical and psychological problems which are entirely out of my control, there is no possible way I

40

can turn you into a competent rider in four weeks, and that unfortunate though it may be, I strongly recommend that they recast the part.'

'You wouldn't do that!'

'You think I wouldn't?'

I knew he would.

'You could try looking at it in a different way.' Angel filled my glass with water in a solicitous manner. 'Being a black widow will be good practice for when they start shooting the serial.'

'A black *widow*!'

'We thought you would make a very fetching black widow,' Anthony said, impassively detaching the last remaining threads of chicken flesh and pushing the bones to the side of his plate. 'The hair plaited into a knot at the nape of the delicate little neck, the oh-so-pretty face pale beneath the spotted veil ...'

This was just too much to take. 'The face certainly will *not* be pale beneath the spotted veil,' I burst out furiously. 'The face won't even be *there*! You are not hiring *me* out as an extra! I won't do it!'

I shot my chair back on the bricks and would have left the table but, as before, Anthony was too quick for me. Once again I felt my upper arm taken in a lock of iron.

'You may as well give in, you know,' Angel said in an exhausted tone. 'You'll have to in the end, so why fight? Anthony won't take no for an answer. He doesn't even recognize the word.' Although her plate was by no means empty, she laid down her knife and fork as if the argument had drained her of the strength necessary to continue eating.

'But it's coercion,' I spluttered angrily. 'Worse than that, it's blackmail!' I tried, without success, to wrench my arm free. I glowered at Anthony.

'I would prefer you to regard it as part of your training

schedule,' he said. 'I would advise you to think of it as a unique and valuable experience. You will possibly even manage to enjoy it. Think of the glamour attached to the making of a film. Imagine yourself watching the top directors at work; meeting the stars ...' He smiled to himself, as if at a private joke. He released my arm.

I slumped back in my chair, defeated. 'It isn't just that I object to doing you a favour, to being made a convenience of, or even missing my riding lesson,' I said in despair. 'It's being hired out as an extra that I really object to.'

'But why?' Over the grisly remains of her supper, Angel regarded me with mild irritation. 'Isn't it quite a good way to gain experience? At least extras get work.'

'But it isn't the right *kind* of work. Actresses don't take work as extras or non-speaking parts, not ever, not if they're *serious*.' I did not really expect Angel to understand, but it was the truth. Ziggy had once warned me about it. 'Don't let anybody talk you into doing crowd scenes, Grace Darling. Nobody ever got lifted out of the ruck to be a star. The only thing an extra ever gets recognition for is being an extra; a piece of human scenery that can't talk, that can't take direction. Extras are a different breed, Kiddo, and don't you forget it.' I had not forgotten it, and much good was it about to do me now.

'I wouldn't worry about being recognized,' Angel said. 'You'll just be a black widow with a veil. There won't be any close-ups.'

It was clear that further argument would be fruitless, but I was not going to be exploited for financial gain as well.

'Will I get paid?' I asked.

Anthony pushed away his empty plate. He tried not to smile.

'*Paid*?' Angel looked pained.

'Now look here,' I said heatedly, 'I know what the rates are and I also know what you are charging Mr Goldstein because I heard you making the arrangements on the telephone. If I *have* to go tomorrow, I'm not giving my services for nothing!'

'Calm down, Grace Darling,' Anthony said. 'You'll get paid.'

'Less our agency discount, of course,' Angel added swiftly. 'After all, you wouldn't be doing the work if it wasn't for us.'

'I wouldn't be doing it at all if I had a choice!' I glared at them both. They grinned back at me. It was infuriating to see them looking so pleased with themselves.

'Eat your supper like a good girl, Grace Darling,' Anthony advised. 'We shall miss breakfast in the morning because we have to be on the road by five.'

'*Five!*'

'Too early for you?' He patted the top of my head as he got up from the table. 'My word, you *do* have a lot to learn about the film business.'

I was still burning with outrage later that evening as I knelt by the little window in the Room of the Costumes, my face cooled by the soft, dew-laden evening air, drenched with the scent of an old honeysuckle clinging precariously to what was left of the plaster. After supper I had helped Angel with what she euphemistically called 'evening stables,' which involved checking every stable, skipping out any droppings, forking over the straw, topping up the water buckets, checking the horses' rugs, and distributing hay nets. I had not disliked these rather domesticated duties, and had found pleasure in the comfortable atmosphere of a stable yard in the evening; the warm, relaxing presence of the horses; the sounds they made; the appreciative nicker at the appearance of a hay net; the scrape of a hoof; the gentle snortings and dribblings in the water buckets. But when Angel had suggested we might look out the harness for the following day and hinted that it might not be clean: 'If I found you a sponge, I don't suppose you could ...' I had drawn the line and stamped back to the farmhouse to bed. Now, of course, I felt rather guilty, and yet I told myself there was no earthly reason why I should. I had done more than my share.

One of the massive front doors banged and Anthony appeared below, walking swiftly towards the woods across the overgrown garden. He was carrying a bottle. I drew back from the window in case he should look up and catch sight of me. In case he should imagine I was spying on him. Where was he going? Was he a secret drinker? Was there a woman waiting for him somewhere in the woods, or in one of the village cottages beyond ? Not that I cared. Not that I was even interested.

Yet it had been Anthony who had insisted on buying the new divan bed. He had wanted me to be miserable in comfort.

Lying under the buttercup yellow duvet, pondering the oddities of fate that had delivered me into his hands like a lamb to the slaughter, that had sent me to bed supperless – I had not been able to stomach the coq au vin and had only managed to dissuade Angel from saving it in the refrigerator by invoking the shade of the Streptococci casserole – and that now promised to make me a black widow at five o'clock in the morning, I fell into a troubled sleep.

6

Waiting at the Church

'... I can't get away
To marry you today,
My wife
Won't let me.'

Anthony appeared to find the situation amusing in a tight-lipped sort of way, but the black horse with the purple plume showed his impatience by digging a hole in the gravel with a front hoof. The activity caused the hearse to tremble violently. Anthony stopped singing and flicked the horse's rump with the end of the reins. The black horse stopped digging and began to throw its head up and down instead, making loud snorting noises. The sun had clouded over. Large drops of rain began to fall.

We had been up by four o'clock to be on the road by five and had reached Pinewood by eleven. On our arrival at the studios we had been redirected to an isolated little church somewhere north of Slough. When we had driven up the rough approach lane we had been met by the Assistant to the Assistant Director; a thin, bearded, anxious-looking individual who had started to berate Anthony for being a few minutes late almost before he was out of the cab. Anthony had retaliated by pointing out that had he been sent a shooting schedule as was the usual procedure, instead of being called out at the last minute by telephone, he could have driven straight to the location instead of being redirected from Pinewood, so the subsequent delay was not his fault.

The heated exchange which followed was almost terminated when Anthony, in the most uncompromising of terms, invited the Assistant to the Assistant Director to procure his hearse from some other party, climbed back into the cab, restarted the engine, and slammed the door in a fine temper, almost detaching several of the AAD's long, tapering fingers which he only managed to snatch away in the nick of time.

After this unpromising start, we were conducted to the make-up caravan with hostility and unseemly haste, but when we had been prepared and costumed to everyone's satisfaction, and had the black horse polished and plumed, harnessed and hitched to the hearse, nobody seemed to want us. The Assistant to the Assistant Director immediately lost interest and vanished amongst the gravestones leaving us abandoned at the lychgate, and now, some two hours later, it had begun to rain.

Perched uncomfortably on the tail end of the hearse in my widow's weeds, I sat under a hideous green plastic umbrella decorated with shocking pink daisies, and waited for Angel to return with coffee from a converted bus parked some way down the approach lane which was dispensing food and drink to the actors and film crew. If my face was pale under the spotted veil it was not only because I had been to make-up, but also because I felt decidedly weak and empty. I had not eaten for twenty-four hours.

All around the ancient little church there was activity of a sort; various members of the thirty-strong film crew, linked to what was happening inside by walkie-talkies, sheltered under the creaking cypress trees; actors in Victorian dress awaited their cues under the green and pink umbrellas handed out by props, some of the women wearing floor-length plastic costume protectors; two video cameras set up on tripods stood swathed in

46

polythene; and cables from the Outside Broadcast Video Unit parked out of sight behind some laurel bushes, snaked across the grass, over and around the weathered tombstones.

The black horse did not like the rain. He fidgeted about, shaking his rain-beaded plume, scattering droplets, and finally shook his whole body in a convulsion which rocked the plywood coffins and precipitated a sheaf of wax lilies into my bombazine lap.

Anthony, wickedly handsome in make-up, having spurned the umbrella offered by props and donned a riding mackintosh and trilby hat, jumped down from the front of the hearse and grimaced up at the sky. He stuck two fingers into his mouth and whistled to attract the attention of the nearest technician. A gestured exchange appeared to indicate that nobody had any idea how long they would take to complete the interior shots, and that nothing could be done outdoors anyway until the rain stopped. Resignedly, he began to unhitch the black horse.

'Come on, Mary Poppins,' he said in a humourless voice, 'let's get the covers on before everything gets soaked.'

'So much for the glamour of filming,' I said irritably as I helped tug a tarpaulin over the hearse. 'So much for watching the top directors at work, and meeting the actors.'

Anthony yanked down his side of the canvas and strapped it to the wheel hubs. He did not reply.

'You knew it would be like this,' I said. 'You expected it.'

Anthony straightened. He gave me one of his customary thin smiles.

'Of course he knew.' Angel appeared at my side, balancing a tin tray on which were three steaming polystyrene containers and a stack of buttered toast. Costumed in narrow black trousers and a sombre frock coat, with her hair scraped up and secured on the top of her head, she had been transformed by make-up into a sunken-cheeked, hollow-eyed boy. 'We once worked on a film for thirteen consecutive days before we even *saw* a camera,' she informed me.

'If we don't see a camera today,' I retorted, 'I won't be seeing one at all on this film because you won't persuade me to come back again.' Never had instant coffee smelled so inviting. I pushed back the spotted veil and took a piece of toast from the stack.

'An actress worth her salt would be prepared to endure a little inconvenience for the sake of her profession,' Anthony said in an acid tone.

'Being hired out against one's will as a piece of human scenery is not my idea of a profession,' I snapped. I took a second piece of toast as an insurance policy. I was not sure when I would see a proper meal. Even the horses were better fed. The black horse had been given a corn feed prior to leaving Moat Farm, he had chewed a hay net during the journey, and now he was comfortably ensconced in the horse box eating another corn feed. When I had complained of hunger, Angel had looked aggrieved. 'You were *offered* food last night,' she had reminded me. 'It wasn't our fault you chose to leave it. You can't blame us.'

Now she led the way into the part of the horse-box vacated by the hearse. We sat on straw bales which had immobilized the wheels during the journey. No sooner had we arranged ourselves than the crunching of heavy wheels upon gravel heralded the arrival of another vehicle, another horse-box.

Anthony swore.

'It's Hender Copper,' Angel said in a low voice. She sounded rather pleased.

Hender Copper was not at all how I had visualized The Enemy. He was short and thickset with ginger hair standing up in a crest and a freckled, rather jolly face. As soon as he had clambered out of the cab, the Assistant to the Assistant Director appeared at his side as if by magic.

'My God, you took your time!' he shouted. 'Noon, I told you! Do you know what noon means? Have you any idea how long we've been waiting? Do you know what time it is now?' He thrust his over-sized wristwatch under Hender Copper's nose. 'It's one o'clock, that's what ruddy time it is!'

'I know what time it is,' Hender Copper protested. 'I've been sitting in a traffic jam for an hour. You've no idea what it's like in Slough at this time of day – all those traffic lights, all at red ...'

'I don't want to listen to any excuses! I want you ready in five minutes, *Mister* Copper. You do know how much time you've got? You know what five minutes means?' In case there was any doubt, the AAD pointed it out in an exaggerated manner on the face of his watch. 'You've got from *there* to *there*, Mister Copper, so you better get a ruddy move on!' He now half-turned and spotted us sitting on the straw bales. 'Well now, this *is* charming, isn't it,' he said in a caustic tone. 'Everybody waiting at the church, and here you are having a nice little tea party ...'

'Breakfast,' Anthony corrected him, 'this is breakfast, not tea. We arrived two hours ago, if you remember. We started out at five and we arrived at eleven fifteen.'

'Anyway, it was raining until a few seconds ago,' I pointed out. 'It has only just stopped.'

'And nobody's waiting,' Angel added, 'they never are. You always say we've kept you waiting, but the only people who have to wait are on our side of the camera. We know that. We weren't born yesterday.'

The AAD gave us a savage look. 'I suppose it would suit you better if the whole bloody film crew were kept waiting on full pay whilst you mess about, arriving when you feel like it, organizing coffee mornings at our expense. I don't suppose you have a clue how much it's costing per hour to shoot this little epic!'

'Oh, I don't know.' Anthony leaned back against the wall of the box in a leisurely manner, tipping the trilby hat over his eyes like a gangster as he considered it. 'You're on video, not film, so that brings the price down a bit; you've got an average strength crew; you've got about twenty actors, no stars that I can see, nobody expensive; and then you've got us – I should say it's under two thousand an hour. It's a fairly low-budget production.'

If this was an accurate calculation, the Assistant to the Assistant Director was not about to give Anthony any credit for it. 'Five minutes, you lot!' he shouted. 'In five minutes I want you ready for shooting outside the ruddy gates!' He hopped off in a frenzy to check that Hender Copper was unloading, then sped off down the lane to reappear a few seconds later dragging a girl in a pink overall clutching a make-up box.

Within ten minutes Hender, made-up and costumed in a layered greatcoat and a top hat, was on the box seat of a hansom cab with a grey horse between the shafts.

'Right,' the AAD shouted, 'where's the bloody widow?'

Did he mean me? I looked up from where I was kneeling unstrapping a corner of the tarpaulin from the hearse wheels.

'Hey, you,' he yelled, 'get in here!' He held open the door of the hansom cab.

I straightened. 'Do you mean me?'

'Of course I mean you!' he screeched. 'Unless we've got more than one widow! Unless the whole ruddy place is crawling with widows!'

'Better do as he says without arguing,' Angel whispered, 'otherwise he's going to twist a gut.'

The girl in the pink overall dusted my nose with white powder, stroked on some lip gloss, and pulled down the spotted veil. I held up the bombazine skirts and gingerly mounted the tiny, wobbly little step into the cab. Before I was halfway, the AAD, deranged with impatience, shoved me from behind and bundled me inside like a piece of baggage. He slammed the door.

Inside the hansom cab everything was black. It was dark, stuffy, claustrophobic, and very spooky. I did not like it. The seat was narrow and uncomfortable. My costume was too hot, the bodice and the sleeves were too tight. I did not know why I had been taken away from the others and put inside the hansom cab. I had no idea what people expected me to do. The whole thing was crazy. I fumbled around for the doorhandle. There did not appear to be one.

Outside, Hendor whipped up the grey horse. The cab lurched forward almost throwing me to the floor. It was too late to get out. I held on to the upholstery. The wheels scraped and crunched along the gravel making an unbelievable noise. The horse's hooves threw up a constant battery of stones against the front of the cab. It sounded like gunfire.

As we passed the hearse I heard the Assistant to the Assistant Director screaming at Anthony to hurry up because everyone was waiting, and Anthony inviting him, in his most relaxed and insolent tone, to have a nice quiet lie down in one of the coffins.

In spite of everything; in spite of the crashing and

splattering gunfire of gravel; in spite of the appalling discomfort; in spite of the restrictive nature of my costume; in spite of the fact that I did not have a clue what was going to happen next, I started to laugh.

All alone in the lurching, jolting hansom cab, deathly pale under the spotted veil, the black widow laughed all the way to the funeral.

7

Bring on the Noddy

The Assistant Director in charge of operations at the lychgate was balding, plump and harassed, dressed half-and-half in Camera Crew Chic and Business Executive Smart which consisted of scuffed suede shoes and washed-out jeans, topped with a Jermyn Street striped shirt yanked open at the neck and an Old Boy tie pulled askew with one end flung over his shoulder.

'Is she a Walk-On or an Extra?' he asked the girl standing next to him as I descended from the carriage. 'Is she just a Noddy?'

The girl with the clipboard consulted her papers. 'She's down as an Extra here, but you could upgrade her, depending on what you want her to do.'

'Depending on how much grey matter she's got up top, you mean.'

'I'm not an idiot,' I protested, 'and I can act. I've got Equity.'

The Assistant Director clutched at his temples. 'Heaven preserve us from an Extra who thinks she can *act*!'

The lychgate was now the scene of frantic activity. Two Riggers were laying tracking rails for the dolly, a wheeled truck which carries the camera and allows it to follow actors as they walk, by the side of the church path. Another two cameras were being set up on either side of the gate. Lighting Engineers were bringing up large sheets of polystyrene used to bounce light, and Sound Engineers were fixing a microphone to the end of a boom mounted on a platform which enabled it to be suspended above the actors, just out of shot.

The hearse arrived in a flurry of gravel with Anthony and Angel up front in their sombre black, wearing top hats with streamers. Within a few seconds Props were busily polishing rain-spots off the bodywork and Make-Up had been summoned with a hair-dryer and extention lead on a rolling drum and were drying off the purple plume and the black horse's mane, both of which were slightly damp. The black horse loathed the drier and pranced about, arching his neck and snorting, but calmed down after receiving a thump on his shoulder from Anthony.

I stood with Hender Copper beside the hansom cab and watched all these goings-on. Anthony had not exchanged a word or even a glance with Hender. As far as each was concerned the other might not have been present. It seemed odd to me that Anthony should indulge in professional jealousy – he did not seem the type to let a little competition worry him – and I could not imagine anyone disliking Hendor for himself because he was friendly and cheerful and obviously popular with the crew. Whilst we waited he told me the story of the hansom cab, how he had found it in a farmyard without any wheels being utilized as a chicken house and how he and the local blacksmith had restored it, how the wheels had been taken from another vehicle, how a local woman had done the upholstery and how it had taken fifty sheets of fine sandpaper and nine separate coats of paint to achieve the mirror-bright finish.

Over the walkie-talkies the voice of the Director could be heard issuing instructions from the OBVU behind the laurels. The cameras on either side of the gate were already rolling, filming establishing shots to iron out any problems before shooting began. The results were appearing on monitors inside the OBVU where the Director was looking at three separate screens recording the output of the cameras from their differing angles. This would continue throughout the filming and later the best shots would be chosen and spliced together to make up the finished film.

The Assistant Director briefed the cameramen as to what was required. 'I want a long shot of the hearse approaching the church, a medium long shot of the driver and the pall-bearer climbing down, then cut to all four bearers shouldering the coffin and a tracking shot as they walk up the path. Cut to a medium shot of the widow being helped out of the cab and a tracking shot of her being supported after the coffin, with a long shot of the rest of the mourners falling in behind. From the camera on the dolly I want a fifty-fifty two shot of the widow and support as they get to the end of the rails, then pan medium long shot to Patrick standing by the stone angel, into close-up and cut. Has everybody got that?' It seemed that everyone had. The Assistant Director now gathered the actors and extras around him for their briefing. There was only one recognizable face amongst the gathering, and that was Patrick Spencer whom I had seen in the West End Theatre and on television. He was a tall, willowy man, pale skinned and blond haired with a bony, rather calculating face. He was usually cast as an upper-crust villain.

The Assistant Director turned first to Anthony. 'I want the hearse to approach the church at a sedate trot and stop at the gate. You stay up top whilst the bearer gets down and joins the others at the rear to shoulder the coffin and walk slowly up the path. Then you move up just enough to let the hansom cab drop the widow at the gate. Got that?'

Anthony nodded.

'You Hender, drive up a way behind the hearse and be ready to move in when he moves along, then stop and hold that position until we're through. OK?' He turned to a rounded man with grey hair and lavishly applied side-burns. 'Ken, as soon as the cab stops, you move forward to open the door and help out the grieving widow and support her up the path after the coffin. The rest of you fall in behind in a seemly procession, and keep the whole thing s-l-o-w. Any questions?'

'Yes,' I said, 'I'd like to know if I'm an Extra or a Walk On.' Everyone looked at me.

The Assistant Director sighed. 'What's your name?'

'Grace Darling,' I said, using my stage name.

'Well now, Grace Darling, you're down as an Extra on my list.'

'I know,' I said, 'but an extra should be a crowd artist and I don't seem to be. Also, an extra doesn't take individual direction and I seem to be playing a specific part.'

'Have I given you individual direction?' the Assistant Director enquired.

'Not to me personally, but I presume I have to act like a bereaved person and allow myself to be helped out of the cab and supported after the coffin. I may even be expected to weep,' I said, 'and that seems like individual direction to me.'

'You're right,' he said.

'Also,' I added, 'if you do want me to weep, I shall need a laced-trimmed handkerchief to weep into, unless you would like me to use a paper tissue.'

'No,' the Assistant Director decided, 'that wouldn't do at all. Fetch Grace Darling a lace-trimmed handkerchief somebody, and change Extra to Walk-On I – she's upgraded as from this minute.'

'Well spoken, Grace Darling,' Patrick Spencer said.

'She'll be wanting an Oscar next,' one of the mourners muttered.

A girl from Costumes returned with a pair of lace panties. 'They're the nearest I can find,' she apologized, 'we seem to be out of lace-trimmed handkerchiefs.'

A shout of laughter went up from the Camera Crew. I took the lace panties with as much dignity as I could muster, feeling my face warming to red. I sensed the Extras who were playing mourners and mutes in the funeral procession, standing huddled together like a flock of black crows, were enjoying my embarrassment, that somehow they felt it served me right for getting myself upgraded.

'OK folks, if we're all ready, let's have a walk-through from the beginning – carriages away!' The Assistant Director despatched everyone to their positions.

At the end of the lane the AAD, in a slightly less hysterical frame of mind, relayed the Director's call for action via his walkie-talkie, setting the black horse off towards the church at a stately trot and timing the interval after which Hendor's cab followed. At the appropriate moment, Ken opened the door and assisted me down the step and after the coffin. I sniffed into the lace panties trying to look suitably distressed, and beside us, the tracking camera on the dolly with the cameraman perched on his little seat was pushed along the rails by a crewmember known as 'the grips'. The mutes fell in behind, and as we walked out of shot, the camera panned to Patrick Spencer standing by the stone angel.

It all seemed very simple and I imagined it would be over in a couple of takes. After all, although the sound engineers were recording the effects – the carriage wheels on the gravel, the horse's hooves, the scrape of the coffin as it slid out of the hearse, and the footfalls of the cortege, nobody had any lines to fluff because nobody had to speak. And as Ken informed me that we were filming the closing sequence of the film and that the credits would be running over us, it did not even seem particularly important in the dramatic sense.

The carriages reassembled at the bottom of the lane for the first take. All went swimmingly until the bearers slid out the coffin and shouldered it.

'It's supposed to be heavy, you ruddy blockheads!' the Assistant Director shouted. 'There's supposed to be a dead weight inside! You can't swing it up like a ruddy fairy cake! Cut!' He waved his hands at the camera crew. 'Cut! Let's take it again from the beginning!'

We all returned to the bottom of the lane. I had not even got out of the cab. On the second take the bearers shouldered the coffin as if it was full of lead, but just as they were setting off up the path to the church a low-flying jet whistled across the sky. The Sound Engineer drew his finger across his throat and everyone trooped back again, stony-faced.

The carriages set off yet again down the drive.

The third take seemed to be perfect until the cameraman on the dolly announced, 'Sorry folks, hair in the gate. Hate to do this to you, but we better have one more try.' This meant that a tiny shred of film had got into the aperture which would appear on the screen as a hair-like filament waving about at the edge. Amidst a chorus of groans, we returned to our starting positions once more.

By this time the grey horse was becoming restive and pranced his way down the drive, lifting his feet up like a hackney with his chin tucked into his chest. Patches of sweat appeared on his neck. This was unseemly behaviour in a horse bearing the chief mourner to a funeral, but as his high-stepping, steaming progress up the lane was unrecorded by the camera, all might have been well had he not plunged forward in an agony of impatience just as

I was about to alight from the cab. As the whole vehicle lurched, my foot caught in my bombazine skirts and missed the step. I flew out of the door and fell straight through Ken's outstretched arms on to the gravel.

'Oh, well *done*, Grace Darling!' the Assistant Director cried. 'Ruddy *beautiful*! Ruddy *marvellous*! Cut everybody! Cut! Cut! Cut! Everybody back to square one!'

'Doing your own stunts as well, dear?' one of the mutes enquired.

Ken helped me to my feet. 'Keep cool,' he said in a low voice, 'take no notice.'

I retrieved the substitute handkerchief from under the cab wheels and gritted my teeth.

'I bet that's the first time she's dropped her knickers for anybody!' another of the mutes shouted gleefully.

Ken pushed me back into the cab as a solid yell of laughter went up. 'Ignore it,' he advised. 'Don't get rattled. For your own sake, keep steady.'

The cab bucketed away with Hendor swearing at the grey horse. I picked gravel out of my gloves. I was shocked and humiliated but I tried to keep cool. I could have wept but I bit my lip instead and clenched my fists. Somehow I managed to be steady.

The fifth take was completed without a single mishap. The fact that my heart was beating like a drum and my hands shook as I was helped out of the hansom cab owed nothing to my acting ability. There was genuine sympathy on Ken's be-whiskered face.

The Assistant Director clapped his hands. 'OK folks, that's the one! It's a wrap!' His attention was immediately captured by his walkie-talkie. 'What wires? Where?' His head swivelled. He stared up at the sky. 'Oh *hell*, Bernard, does it really *show*?' He turned back to us, agonized. 'I hardly know how to say this folks, but it seems we've got a telephone wire just tipping through one corner of number three camera. We'll have to do it one more time. Everybody take thirty whilst props get some dingle organized.'

There was a collective moan of anguish. The bearers shoved the coffin resignedly back into the hearse. Anthony unhitched the black horse. Hendor drove the cab off towards his horsebox. Ken excused himself and went off in search of the portacabin loo. The Assistant Director sent props to purloin branches from nearby trees in order to mask the wire. The mutes flocked, but the black widow was left alone on the church path.

'Allow me to escort you to the restaurant, Grace Darling.' Patrick Spencer, lean, elegant, and decidedly sinister in his make-up, proffered his arm. The mutes flapped and gaped.

The bus, a double-decker, was properly fitted with tables and seating, a galley kitchen and servery. 'Shall we go up to the terrace?' Patrick Spencer settled me to a table on the upper deck and provided coffee and mountainous scones. 'Especially baked to banish stomach rumblings on the set, with a miracle ingredient guaranteed to cure anyone afflicted by the trots due to stagefright.' I did not believe him, but managed to smile. The black crows flocked nearby, fluttering their disapproval, making it clear they considered that studio etiquette was being breached.

'I hear you're staying with the King.' From the pocket of his frock coat, Patrick Spencer produced a gold lighter, an ivory cigarette holder and a packet of Black Sobrane. He held them up to the crows. 'Rather appropriate for a funeral, don't you think?'

The crows tried to smile.

'The King?' I sipped the coffee, appreciating its comforting warmth, grateful that Patrick Spencer had placed himself firmly on my side.

'In the business he's known as The King of the Horsemasters.'

I realized he was referring to Anthony. I nodded. I looked at the miraculous scone and wondered whether I could tackle it. I decided I could. I unbuttoned my gloves.

'Well, if you have to learn how to handle horses, there certainly isn't anyone better to learn from.' Extracting a cigarette from the packet, he inserted it into the holder. 'You know he was responsible for all the horse scenes in Sternberg's *Black Beauty*?'

I had not known, but I remembered the film. It had been heartbreakingly realistic. Audiences who had not hitherto known what a bearing rein was had left the cinema aware of its cruelty, deploring the fate of the cab-horses, puffy-eyed over the death of poor Ginger. I cut into the scone.

'I had only a minor part consisting of three short scenes.' Patrick Spencer lit the black cigarette and leaned his blond head backwards, taking a long draught, watching the smoke as it rose towards the roof as he exhaled it. 'But I shall never forget the way he handled those horses. It was simply incredible, especially the fire scenes. He actually worked them in the smoke, amongst the flames – they were terrified, you could see that, yet they trusted him implicitly. There is no doubt that the man is an absolute genius.'

I buttered half a scone and took a bite. Instantly I realized that I was famished. Due to the absolute genius, I had not eaten for almost two days.

'Of course, we all know he can be difficult. Take *Total Eclipse* for an example. I was not in the film, but I worked with Teresa Sanderson soon afterwards, and I know what happened there.'

'What did happen there?' Almost restored by the

coffee and now on the second half of the scone, I looked across at him, interested.

'Teresa Sanderson was the female lead. She was playing Stella – I don't know if you are familiar with the film? As you know, Teresa is quite a name, she has drawing power and she knows it. She also fancies herself as a horsewoman, and she made it a condition of the contract that she did all the mounted scenes. There were to be no stand-ins, no stunt riders for her part, she was going to do it all herself. Naturally, the King demurred, but there was not a lot he could do about it.' With a smile, the second scone was pushed over to my side of the table. 'Do please eat mine, I beg you. I much prefer to smoke and I abhor waste.'

'Well ... if you are absolutely sure you don't want it. I did miss breakfast.' Gratefully I took the scone and returned his smile. 'What happened next?'

'Things were fine for a few days, but then a gargantuan row broke out over a scene in which one of the horses had to jump over a wall with three strands of barbed wire on the top.'

'It wouldn't have been real barbed wire, surely?'

'It could have been faked easily enough, but the King wouldn't let his horse jump fake wire which would have broken the minute he touched it, because he said when it met the real thing the horse wouldn't respect it, wouldn't realize it could almost take its leg off. So although the barbs were silver-painted rubber, the wire was real.'

I had not seen the film. 'Was it a high wall?' I sliced into the second scone. Patrick Spencer stubbed out his first cigarette even though it was only half smoked, and removed it from the holder.

'It was a good height. I believe they started off with a low one, built it up brick by brick until it was at the maximum height for the horse to manage comfortably, then angled the camera to make it look an impossible feat.' He lit the fresh cigarette, sucking in cheeks made cadaverous by make-up, looking like a death's head. 'Jumping wasn't Teresa's strong point. When the King saw how she rode the horse at the wall, he demanded a stunt-rider.'

'Did they give him one?'

'They did not. Teresa was adamant and she won. There was a blistering row, but the King was forced to capitulate. He schooled her apparently, and gave precise instructions on how she should approach the obstacle, but somehow she became confused, lost her nerve, who knows? The result was that the horse went through the wire instead of over it – with disasterous consequences.'

I put down my scone. 'It didn't have to be shot, did it? It didn't break a leg?'

'No, but it was badly gashed. The King went berserk. He socked the AD, snatched all the horses off the set, loaded them into his wagon and left, right in the middle of the film. You can imagine the confusion. The whole film revolves around the horses and nobody knew what to do. Poor old Hender was called in, but how could he cope? He hasn't the horses, and to be perfectly frank, he hasn't the talent either. To salvage the film they had to persuade the King to come back and his condition was that they recast the female lead.'

'You mean get rid of Teresa Sanderson?' My mind flew back to the previous evening, when the coq au cochineal and the flaccid, glistening chips lay congealing on my plate, when Anthony said 'And I could tell them how uncooperative you are … how inept in the saddle … and that I strongly recommend that they recast the part.' And I was small beer compared with Teresa Sanderson. 'Did he succeed?'

'They had to do it. There was no other way. Teresa was

paid off, Camilla Lee was brought in, and the King's sister – Angelica, I believe her name is – did the stand-in and stunt riding.'

'That's quite a story.'

'But then he is quite a character.'

At that moment a fluttering amongst the crows heralded the arrival of the King himself at the top of the stairs. Over Patrick Spencer's elegantly caped shoulder I watched as he took a seat, removed his trilby hat, lodged a boot on the opposite seat. It was amazing how make-up had enhanced his brooding looks. He could have been Valentino, his eyes were so dazzlingly brilliant.

'I like you, Grace Darling,' Patrick Spencer said in his lazy, cultured voice. 'I have been watching you today and you show promise. You also have spirit. But if you are going to work with the King on a film, you have to watch your step. Do not get involved. Do not become familiar. He might play with you in the way a cat plays with a mouse, he is capable of that, but you must appreciate that he cares for nobody, for nothing, other than for his horses. Keep your distance. Remember if you as much as scratch one of his precious equines, he will be merciless.'

I looked at Patrick Spencer. Over his caped shoulder I was aware of Anthony looking steadily at me. Despite the stuffy atmosphere and my many-layered costume, I felt a chill run down my back. The hairs pricked on the back of my neck.

Patrick Spencer was now attending to his third Black Sobrane. 'Every now and again, Grace Darling,' he said between puffs, 'remind yourself of what happened on *Total Eclipse*. Remember that history has a way of repeating itself. Take care.'

'Thank you for the advice. I'm grateful for it.' Suddenly the upper deck seemed unbearably claustro-phobic. I wanted to get away from Patrick Spencer and his unwonted advice, from the exotic smell of his cigarettes, from the black crows, rustling their jealous feathers because the star was paying attention to a Walk-On. But most of all I wanted to get away from Anthony, who cared for nobody, who looked like Valentino but had a heart as impermeable as granite. I got up from my seat.

'Mr Spencer ... Thank you for everything ... Now I have to go to Make-up ...'

I pulled down the spotted veil, held up my skirts and left without a glance to left or right. Once out of the chuck wagon I decided to go back to the horse-boxes in search of Hender, but when I found him he was passionately engaged on the straw bales with one of the boys who were acting as pall-bearers.

I fled before either spotted me. I was not unfamiliar with homosexuality because it was quite widespread in the theatrical world. Many of the male students at the Rose Jefferson Academy where I had done my drama training had been that way inclined and the landlord of Henry Irving House where I had lodged for the last year had been not only gay but also outrageously camp. So I knew all about that side of life.

But somehow it didn't seem right to see Hender embracing a boy. I was half-way to Make-up before I realized that his lover had not been a boy at all. It had been Angel.

8

The Path Through the Woods

'Angel,' I said, 'when was the last time the Aga was lit?'

She thought about it. 'Last winter. No, later than that because it was such a cold spring. May, I think.'

'Could we light it now?'

The cobalt eyes widened. 'What on earth for?'

'I just thought ... if it was lit, we might have more constant hot water – we could also cook.'

'Cook?' Angel's eyebrows rose. 'We?'

'Well,' I remembered the streptococci casserole. '*I* could. I'm not fantastic, but I could do better than the *Hare and Hounds*. If I have to face another slimy chip, I think I shall die.'

Angel looked at me. She looked at the Aga. Cookery was something she had never suggested. I had half expected it; the mixture of hope and speculation on her face, the hesitant way she would begin 'I don't suppose ... if I found you a saucepan – in your spare time ...?' It had never happened. But now I had suggested it, she warmed to the idea at once.

'There is some *fuel* in the outhouse ...'

'So you wouldn't mind if I went ahead?'

'It isn't all that easy to light. You need kindling – paper and sticks for a start. You will have to nurse it. Someone will have to keep it fed.'

'I shall nurse it. I shall keep it fed. There are plenty of old *Horse and Hounds* lying about. I can collect sticks from the wood.'

'I wouldn't go into the wood,' Angel said hastily. 'It

might not be safe. Undesirable types from the village tend to lurk. You know, poachers and people like that.'

I was not intimidated by the thought of a poacher or two, not after the undesirables one encountered in Soho, but I was touched by her unexpected regard for my personal safety. 'All right,' I agreed, 'I'll collect sticks from the edge of the wood.'

'You will need something to cook with.'

'There are saucepans and things in the bottom of the dresser. I've looked.'

'Not saucepans. Food. Ingredients.'

'We could go to the supermarket in the village. We could call there during our ride.' Now into my second week at Moat Farm I was now having a lunge lesson early in the morning, a school lesson at noon, and a hack in the afternoon. 'I want to call at the Post Office anyway, to ask about my script.'

'I thought you had given up worrying about the script,' Angel said crossly. 'There's no point in badgering the Post Office. We keep telling you all sorts of things can go wrong with scripts. People have died waiting for scripts to arrive.'

'Well I'm not going to die waiting for mine to arrive,' I snapped. 'If it isn't here by the beginning of next week I'm going to ring my agent and find out what has happened.' As a matter of fact I had already tried to ring Ziggy several times, but the telephone at the Café Marengo seemed to be permanently engaged.

'There's no point in ringing your agent,' Angel insisted, 'he won't be able to tell you anything. You heard what Anthony said ...'

'I don't *care* what Anthony said! Nor does he care if the script arrives or not! Anthony attaches no importance to what I do! He disapproves of me! He makes that very clear!'

I looked at Angel in aggravation. She sat on the kitchen table wearing the inevitable jeans and suede chaps, swinging her jodhpur-booted feet, with her extravagant hair caught up in two bunches above her ears like a King Charles spaniel. 'It's only because you want to be an *actress*,' she said. 'You know how he hates actors and actresses.'

'Almost as much as he hates film producers and directors! He seems to hate everyone in the profession! Sometimes I wonder why he stays in the business!' But of course, I knew why he stayed. It was because of the horses. He was their protector. Their champion. He stayed to be the conscience of every actor who ever made use of a horse for the camera, of every stunt rider, every producer, every director. And he had a very long memory. Other people remembered Borodino, Glencoe, Belsen, Hiroshima. Anthony remembered *Ben Hur*.

'So you don't fancy him?' Angel said.

I stared.

'Most women do, you know. They find him fascinating.'

'I'm not most *women*!' I did not want to discuss Anthony's fascinating effect on the opposite sex. I opened one of the doors on the front of the Aga. Ash trickled on to the kitchen floor. 'I'm an *actress*!' I slammed the door shut.

'It *is* an obstacle, one has to admit.'

'And I do not *fancy* Anthony!'

'No, of course not. I can't think why I mentioned it.' Angel countered my glare with a totally guileless look. She jumped down from the table. 'We could ride to the village now, if you like, or would you prefer to light the Aga first?'

'I can light the Aga later,' I said grumpily. 'It will take all night to warm up so I won't be able to cook until tomorrow, but we can do the shopping, and we can call at the *Hare and Hounds* to cancel the meals after this evening.'

'So we don't need to go to the Post Office?'

'We *do* need to go to the Post Office!'

'There's no need to be so prickly,' she said in a reproving tone. 'I'm only trying to save you another disappointment.'

Her confident pessimism was infuriating. I said irritably, 'You seem so certain my script isn't going to arrive that I'm beginning to wonder if you know something about ATC that I don't.'

'Know something about ATC?' Angel paused in the kitchen doorway, the cobalt eyes were wide and innocent. 'Oh no, Grace. I can assure you I know nothing whatsoever about ATC. Nothing at all.'

I almost believed her.

There was no script waiting for me at the Post Office. I had not really expected that there would be.

In the supermarket I shopped for chops and salad, cheese and fruit – easy things. Bread, milk, eggs and dairy produce were delivered daily to Moat Farm. I staggered to the check-out further encumbered by a five-pound pack of new potatoes and a litre of white wine.

Angel waited outside with the horses. We had brought the lunge-lesson pony as a pack animal. His panniers were historic accoutrements dating from the era of Roundheads and Cavaliers. They were not at all commodious. The leather was cracked and the stitching weak. The potatoes and the wine were heavy items and I was not confident that the panniers would hold out.

'We shall have to take the short way back through the woods,' Angel decided. She was riding a tall, speckled grey horse with a noble Roman nose and a high head carriage. I was riding the roan with the long, white stockings who had been loose because he liked to be loose on the day I arrived. Angel leaned down and put some weight on the offside stirrup whilst I mounted. I had not yet mastered the art of swinging lightly and easily into the saddle. My muscles were still protesting too much for me to try.

It was the first time I had been taken into the woods, and yet the horses were clearly accustomed to the path which was well-worn by countless hooves. It was the obvious route to and from the village, avoiding the narrow, twisting lane with its black hedges and steeply rising banks where there was precious little room to escape the unexpectedly rocketing car, or road-hogging tractor belching blue smoke.

Angel led the way, leading the pack pony. The wood was thick, dark and silent. Our horse's hooves made little sound other than where the mud of the winter had baked to a dry crust. Twigs snapped, old leaves rustled, leather creaked, as we followed the path that Anthony had taken on the first night when I had watched from my window; and yes, I had seen him again and again, crossing the wilderness in the dusk with a bottle under his arm. I had never managed to stay awake long enough to hear him return.

We rode past a cottage, tumbledown, almost a ruin, with slipping thatch and cracked walls green with lichen and covered with ivy and deadly nightshade, looking like a stage set for a sinister scene in a pantomime. Only one window retained any glass. I fancied something moved behind it, then realized it must have been my own reflection.

'What a sad little place! Who does it belong to?'

Angel applied her heels to the speckled grey, as if to hasten past as quickly as possible. I remembered her warning about the wood not being safe and wondered if the cottage was a rendezvous for the undesirables she had mentioned.

'It belongs to us. But it's quite derelict. Absolutely uninhabitable. Don't ever come here. It's dangerous.'

'As if I would!' This time there was no suggestion that '... we might do it up ... get a new roof ... treat the beams ...'

Angel looked round. 'Shall we trot on? Do you feel confident?' Without waiting for a reply she sent the speckled grey into trot.

As the roan horse trotted steadily behind, I kept a wary eye on the panniers. I could rise easily to the trot by now and no longer had to strain to keep in time with the gait. Nor did I need to use the reins as a life-line now that the lunge-lessons were beginning to have their effect, deepening and strengthening my seat, improving my balance. Already I was beginning to look and feel like a rider.

I leaned forward and rubbed the roan's neck with my knuckles and he flipped an ear backwards by way of acknowledgement. Our partnership was unequal as yet, but we were partners all the same. I knew I had Angel to thank for this. For all her oddly uncomfortable ways, she had proved an able instructress and whatever I had achieved in such a short time was really her success, not mine. As the path widened and the trees became less dense, it was possible to ride three abreast.

'Whatever happens to me as an actress,' I said, 'I shall always be grateful to you for teaching me to ride and love horses.'

Across the pack pony with his creaking, historic panniers, Angel looked at me in a censorious manner. 'I can only teach you how to ride,' she said. 'If you are learning to love horses then that must be regarded as a bonus. You can't teach a person to love. Nobody can. It just happens. It comes from inside.'

This was true. And yet I thought it difficult for a person to ride and know horses without also learning to love them. And it seemed to me it was a very special sort of love, very pure, very unselfish, because a horse could not *really* love you back, in your heart you knew that. Horses were not blindly faithful, affectionate animals like dogs; yet they were strong and beautiful, fast and courageous, and willing – even eager – to co-operate, having no expectations other than fair treatment. 'I have never understood before why people loved horses,' I said, 'but I understand it now.'

We rode through the thinning trees, towards the wilderness, on a path made flat and dusty by steel-shod hooves and the soles of long, brown boots treading it in the moonlight. Going where? To see whom?

'Sometimes I think it's a pity that loving horses isn't quite enough.'

'Isn't enough?' It seemed a surprising comment from someone whose whole world revolved around them.

'Loving people is far more complicated,' Angel said.

'I know what you mean.'

'Do you?'

'Yes. It can't be easy, juggling Anthony and Hender Copper.'

Instantly, I wished I had not said it. Angel's face froze. 'I don't believe I know what you mean,' she said.

There was no retracting it now. 'You do. You may as well admit it. I saw you together when we were filming.'

'You saw me with Hender Copper? No, you were mistaken.' Angel stared stiffly ahead.

'There was no mistake. You know perfectly well you were with him in the back of the horse-box. I saw you.'

'You mean you were watching! You were spying on us!' Having decided there was no further point in denial, Angel now reined in the speckled grey, aghast, enraged.

'I didn't watch, and I certainly didn't spy. I just happened to come back to the box unexpectedly. I couldn't believe it at first, but then I realized why Anthony is so antagonistic towards Hender. It must be very difficult.'

'Difficult!' Flushed with anger, Angel pounced on the word like an angry terrier.

'Well of course it must be *difficult*.' Over the lunge-lesson pony standing patiently on the path, I looked at her in exasperation. 'If you wanted to make the relationship with Hender permanent, Anthony would be left to run this place on his own. Then Hender would have the benefit of your experience and expertise, and you would be rivals for the same business – brother and sister!'

'And I suppose you think I haven't considered that!'

'I know you must have considered it.'

We looked at each other in silence for a while. The pack pony closed his eyes. The speckled grey sighed and rested a hindleg. The roan with the white stockings stood like a rock and stared into the distance.

'Every girl who has ever worked in the yard has been a threat to me,' Angel said. 'Every time I wondered what would happen if Anthony fell in love. I didn't know how I would cope with that. I was frightened of being displaced, of being left out. Anthony may not be very sociable, he may be obsessed about his horses, he may be difficult, but he was all I had and I dreaded having to share him with somebody else. And now?' She looked at me and to my dismay the beautiful cobalt eyes overflowed with despair. 'Now I don't know what to do.'

Luckily, one of the panniers chose this moment to split, spraying the path with new potatoes, startling the horses. It was a welcome diversion. Because I could not afford to involve myself in an emotional issue between Angel and Anthony, I knew that. It was too potentially dangerous. Anthony was dangerous. And I had my career to think of.

Yet as I chased after potatoes in the wilderness, I had the sneakiest feeling that I was already involved right up to my neck.

9

One Day, For a Million Reasons ...

'Isn't that rather cruel?'

On my way back from the postbox at the end of the drive where once again I had failed to find not only my script, but any post at all, Angel having beaten me to it as usual, I stopped at the giant sandpit in which Anthony was training a brown horse with unexpected splashes of white on its rump.

One of the horse's front legs had been strapped up and as it balanced on three legs, Anthony slowly pulled the opposite rein over the saddle, bending its head backwards until it was forced to slide down on to its strapped knee. Further pressure on the rein caused the horse to collapse on to its side.

'Well, *isn't* it?'

Anthony, deftly unstrapping the leg and releasing the rein so the horse could scramble to its feet and be rewarded with oats, gave me an irritated look.

'I thought you were having a lesson,' he said shortly.

'I've had it.'

I was now having one lunge-lesson and two school lessons a day. It was exhausting and made me sore, but as Angel pointed out, four weeks was not long enough to become proficient in comfort, and so it had to be endured.

'Well,' I said again, '*is* it cruel?'

Anthony walked the brown horse round the sandpit a few times then knelt to restrap the leg. He wore khaki breeches with long brown boots and a black shirt with the sleeves rolled above his elbows. He had not bothered to shave and as he leaned over the straps his dark hair fell into his eyes. He pushed it back with an impatient gesture. Without make-up he looked more like an itinerant horse-coper than Rudolph Valentino which was something of a relief.

'Everything is cruel to start with,' he said in a testy voice. 'Putting a collar and lead on a puppy is cruel to begin with; sending a child to school on the first day is cruel if you care to think of it like that. In any case,' he gave me a narrow look, 'since when have you been interested in the welfare of my horses.'

I was not prepared to rise to this. I had made up my mind not to be in any way provocative or contentious, but on the other hand, nor was I prepared to be intimidated.

'What are you doing exactly?'

He straightened. 'I'm teaching him to fall, if you must know. I'm without a faller at the present and I have to start again from scratch.'

'What happened to the last one?'

He passed the rein over the saddle. 'The last what?'

'The last faller. Did you sell it?'

'You don't *sell* a faller!' From the brown horse's shoulder he looked at me in exasperation. 'For your information, Grace Darling, fallers are like gold dust. It takes a very special sort of horse to become a faller, and they don't come along all that often. It's a tough job and hard on the limbs. A good faller will fall for you hundreds, perhaps thousands of times, but then one day, for a million reasons, he won't fall when you ask him, and that will be the end of it.'

'Which one of the million reasons did your faller stop for?'

He slackened the rein, resigned now to having to answer my question. The brown horse waited, expectant and slightly anxious, nosing the strapped foreleg, looking perplexed. 'Shoulder lameness. There was nothing discernable at first, nothing to see, nothing to explain it. She seemed perfectly sound, absolutely level. But gradually the weakness began to show itself and it never left her. She never worked again.'

'She? Isn't it unusual for a mare to make a faller?'

'Yes, but she was the best faller in the business in her time.'

'And will he be a good faller?' I looked at the brown horse. The brown horse looked at Anthony, waiting for something to happen.

'He might, if you buzz off and let me get on with it. At least he's shaping up better than the others I've tried.'

I was not going to be dismissed just like that. I sat down on one of the sleepers which prevented the sand from spreading over the paddock. 'I think I would rather like to stay and watch. Observation is part of my educational programme, or so I was told.'

'My God, you're persistent.' He turned his back.

This time the horse knew what was going to happen and resisted, attempting to drag his head away from the rein, opening his mouth in an effort to drop the bit, leaning on Anthony, and finally trying to rise up on to his hind legs, but Anthony was strong and the rein relentless. Eventually he slid down on to his knee and rolled over on to the sand. He was not released immediately, but made to lie there, praised with soothing words as he lay. After the unbuckling came the oats and another walk round the sandpit. This time the other foreleg was strapped and this time the brown horse went down as sweetly as a lamb.

'Do horses fall more naturally one way than the other?'

'Don't you *ever* give up? All horses are one-sided, you

will find that out for yourself eventually. Usually it stems from their breaking, people tend to lunge them more the way they go best. But if you think about it, they are usually handled from one side, led and mounted, girthed and bridled, and all the time the horse has its head bent towards the handler, stretching the muscles on the opposite side, using them, making them more elastic. One sidedness is a physical thing, muscular, nothing to do with disobedience.'

'I see.'

'Do you?' The voice was sceptical.

'Yes, I do. You explained it perfectly. It's only logical.'

He fed the brown horse oats, walked it round again. 'If you've grasped that fact, Grace Darling, you'll have done more than the majority of riders. If you bother to notice, you'll see them all the time, trying to cure one-sidedness by force, dragging the horse by the mouth, tightening the side-reins ...'

'No wonder your horses love you.' It was a spontaneous compliment, genuine.

He looked round at me in surprise, arrested in the strapping of a foreleg. For a fleeting moment he was Valentino again, totally devastating, but just as swiftly the moment had passed. He resumed strapping the foreleg. He stood up and passed the rein over the brown mane streaked with white hairs. I watched as the brown horse sank to one knee, powerless to resist. He rolled on to his side in the sand. One felt it was against his will but there was nothing he could do about it.

On the way back to the stables, the brown horse walked between us.

'How will you get him to fall at the gallop with a rider in the saddle?' I asked.

'He won't fall at the gallop. I don't allow it. Eventually I shall get him to fall from a canter and they will

78

undercrank the camera to speed up the action. After a few more sessions he should begin to fall to the rein aid before he has to. Some horses never reach that point and if they don't you know they will never make it. You can't force it, they have to fall willingly. When he falls to the rein aid I'll get on top, we'll start falling from a walk, and work up to canter. It's surprisingly easy from canter because it's three-time, you've got a leading leg and you can put the horse in the right position.'

'But in front of the camera, he'll be falling on hard ground.'

'No horse of mine falls on hard ground. I get the place prepared beforehand. I know where the camera is. I know exactly where he has to fall.'

I looked at the brown horse with the grey hairs in his mane and I wondered how many times he would fall for the camera. Hundreds? Thousands? Before one day, for a million reasons, he wouldn't do it any more. 'It all seems so ... unnecessary.'

'Unnecessary it may be, but as long as film people want horses to fall for entertainment, somebody has to make sure they can do it without hurting themselves.' We stopped outside a stable door. 'Don't tell me you're getting soft, Grace Darling. Starting to consider the horses.'

It was a barb, and typical of Anthony, but perhaps it was one I deserved. I was no longer the same person who had ridden the Raven at the film test. Already Moat Farm had changed all that. I stroked the brown horse's face. 'I'm getting to know them I suppose. And once you do ... when you know what they're like ... it's not very easy to explain, but there's something about horses ... the way they are, that catches your heart.'

'In that case, perhaps I should introduce you to the

mare who was once the best faller in the business.' He opened the half-door.

I looked at the bay mare with the gentle eyes and the satin coat, and at the hugely swollen stomach which seemed too big for her slender black legs to carry. 'But I know this mare, I feed her every morning. She's in foal.'

'It seemed a good idea. The lameness won't go away, but it isn't acute.'

'So she was your famous faller. Will she foal whilst I'm here? Will I see the foal?'

'You can attend the happy event if you want to. She's due any time. That's why she's in the foaling box.'

'I think I would rather not. I would probably faint.' I looked around the foaling box, expecting to see something, I was not sure what.

'There's nothing to see. It isn't exactly a labour ward. It's just bigger than the other boxes, there's more room, and less risk of her getting cast.'

'Cast?'

'Wedged with her legs folded against the wall. Horses do get themselves in that position sometimes when they roll over. Then they start to panic because they can't move.'

I went inside the stable, up to the mare. She rubbed her face against my shirt. She was very beautiful. 'When her foal is old enough to train, will it be a faller?'

Anthony came into the box, the brown horse stood outside with the rein on the ground, as it was trained to do. 'If it's a colt, I will try it. If it's a filly, I'm not so sure. I don't know if it's a good idea to use a mare as a faller, I don't know that they're tough enough.'

I put my arms around the mare's satin neck. 'Then I hope she has a filly.'

'You *are* getting soft!'

'I know what you are thinking. Who am I to criticize?

I'm only an actress! Worse, I'm the stupid bitch who only cared about getting the part, who didn't know the first thing about riding, who lamed The Raven for five weeks. I realize I shall never live *that* down!'

Anthony did not deny it. He did not even look at me. He put his hands in the pockets of his breeches and he leaned against the wall of the foaling box. He stared through the open door. It seemed impossible to reach him, but it was the perfect opportunity to say what I had been thinking.

'Hender Copper's got a faller.'

The texture of the silence suddenly changed. Now it was terrible. Ominous. But I had begun and there was nothing to it but to continue.

'You do *know* about Angel and Hender. You can't go on ignoring it. Sooner or later you are going to have to do something about it!'

'And sooner or later, you are going to have to keep your nose out of things that don't concern you!'

'Angel concerns me!' I cried. 'Don't ask me why because I won't have an answer, but somehow she does *concern* me!'

'And you think she doesn't concern *me*?'

I sighed. 'I don't think anything concerns you, apart from your horses.'

'You are very good at dishing out unwanted advice,' Anthony said in a thin voice.

'You do need a faller,' I said.

Now he looked at me and the eyes were pure Valentino. 'Grace Darling, have you always been so bloody *infuriating*?'

I had to look away. 'I suppose so. Just as you have always been so perfectly hateful.'

He moved across the straw. I closed my eyes. I did not want him to come near me.

'Do you *really* hate me?'

What could I say that would not be a lie? 'I'm trying,' I said.

He lifted a hand to my face. I must have flinched because with the back of it he rubbed my cheek, as gently, as soothingly as if I was one of his horses.

'Keep hating me, Grace Darling,' he said. 'Somehow I think it would be better for everyone.'

10

Where Do You Go To, My Lovely?

'He will never agree,' Angel said.

'He might.'

'You mean you have actually mentioned it!'

'Yes.'

'When!'

'Yesterday.'

'And what was his reaction? What did he say!'

I moved the potatoes, boiling furiously, to a cooler spot on the Aga hotplates. 'Very little actually.'

'I *bet* he did!' Angel paced the kitchen, looking fraught.

'But he didn't dismiss the idea! He didn't *refuse*! Listen Angel, he does *know*, so I wasn't giving away any great secret. Anthony is no fool. And it makes perfect *sense* because you would all benefit. You would have Hender who would be a great help in the yard, nobody can deny he's a great worker – you only have to look at the work he put in on the hansom cab to see that; Anthony would have a faller and some more driving horses, and Hender would benefit from Anthony's skill and from not having to rent a yard; but the greatest advantage would be that you would all be working for the same team – where is the problem?'

'Anthony is the problem.' Angel said darkly.

We both fell silent, thinking about Anthony. I put a frying pan on the Aga and put into it a little oil and butter. I sprinkled the pork chops with pepper and lemon juice.

'Anthony would be the greatest *beneficiary*,' I said.

'But how do we get him to see that? What is the next step?'

'We all sit down and discuss it. We shall invite Hender to supper.'

'Invite Hender to supper!' Angel stopped pacing and looked aghast. 'Anthony will eat him alive!'

The oil and butter began to sizzle. I put the chops into the pan. 'No he won't. In any case there is more to Hender than you give him credit for. Do it, Angel. Go and see Hender and sell him the idea. Ask him for supper. It may not work, it could be a disaster, but at least you will *know*, Angel. It's worth a *try*!'

Angel flopped down into a chair. 'Yes,' she conceded. 'It is worth a try.'

'I don't suppose Anthony has any attachments himself?' I tried to keep my voice casual.

'Attachments?'

'I wondered where he goes to, at nights.' I kept my back to her. Turned the chops.

'At nights?' Angel's voice sounded furtive.

'I've seen him go into the woods from my bedroom window ... a few times – accidentally, of course.'

'Of course.' Angel was playing for time. She must *know* where he went.

'I just thought, if he did have someone, it would make it easier to understand your relationship with Hender.' It sounded rather unlikely, even to my own ears.

'I don't know where he goes. Perhaps to the *Hare and Hounds* for a few drinks.'

'With his own bottle?'

'Look, if you want to know anything about Anthony, you had better ask him yourself.' Angel now turned defensive. 'Anyway, why do you want to know? I thought you weren't interested.'

'I'm not.'

'Hrmmm.' The tone was disparaging. 'Because of Richard?'

'Yes.'

'Ha!'

I was not about to be drawn on the subject of Richard. I was waiting for him to ring. I needed his help. Both Anthony and Angel regarded my anxiety about the non-arrival of my script as premature, but it was week three at Moat Farm and by now I was really worried. I suspected that something had gone wrong. Earlier in the day I had tried to telephone Ziggy again, and this time, instead of getting the engaged tone, all I had heard was a continuous burring sound. On application to the Operator I had been told that the number had been withdrawn from service. When I had asked what that meant, I had been referred to Directory Enquiries. After a goodly interval, Directory Enquiries had informed me that the number I had been trying to dial had been changed and was now listed as Ex-Directory. I had explained that as the Café Marengo was a Soho café this was impossible. Directory Enquiries had snapped that it was not only possible but fact. Bewildered and apprehensive, I had replaced the telephone receiver.

I did not know what was happening at the Café Marengo but I did not like the sound of it. Panic had begun to stir. I needed to find Ziggy, to talk to him urgently. Why had he not tried to contact me? Should I ring Richard and beg him to take me to London? I had decided to wait one more day and if he had not telephoned by then, I would take the initiative. I did not want to do it. Richard already felt himself used and, however cleverly I phrased it, I would be compromised. There would be no pulling the wool over his eyes. But I had to get to London, and if I had to beg, then I would beg. I was resigned to that.

'What's this?'

Anthony now appeared at the kitchen door. He looked astonished.

'What is *what*?' Thinking about my script and Richard and the mystery of the Café Marengo had made me feel stressed. There was also the problem of Angel and Hendor. Then there was Anthony, who sometimes looked like Valentino, who was capable of playing cat and mouse and who could have me thrown off the set and out of the television serial if I so much as put a toe out of line. On top of all this, I was sore and exhausted from the increased riding lessons and worried that I would not be good enough to please Tom Sylvester. It was a bad moment.

'You're cooking!'

'You knew I was going to cook,' I said crossly. 'I told you last night. Why else would I have lit the Aga.'

Anthony looked at me. His eyes widened.

'You've washed the floor!'

'It was disgustingly filthy.'

'There are plates on the dresser!'

There were. All my frustrations had been vented in an orgy of washing, cleaning, scrubbing and tidying. The bricks on the floor were no longer a uniform mud-colour, but revealed in shades ranging from cream to rose. Spiders' webs and the dusty husks of their victims had been banished from the beams overhead. The converted oil lamp gleamed. The Aga threw out a companionable warmth. Old, unmatched plates pleased the eye on the dresser, and the table was laid for supper with salad and cheese and french bread. The kitchen was a different place.

'What have you done with all my letters, my bills?'

'They are in the office.'

'You haven't started to clear out the office!'

'No.'

'Thank God for that!'

I had hardly expected him to be grateful. He now picked up the bottle of wine. 'Anjou Blanc. Three pounds ninety nine pence. I bet its absolutely terrible.'

'It isn't. I've tasted it.'

'*Have* you?'

'I used half a glass for the gravy.'

'Is there no end to your talents, Grace Darling?'

I snatched the potatoes off the hotplate and took them to the stone sink to drain. I was in no mood for badinage. There were to be no cat and mouse games between Anthony and myself. Patrick Spencer had warned me about that.

'As long as I am here, I shall do the cooking,' I told him. 'My stomach won't take any more meals on wheels, and if you don't like the idea, I suggest you take yourself off to eat at the *Hare and Hounds*!'

It was spoken in temper and a chancy thing to say to someone like Anthony, but he took it in surprisingly good part. He unscrewed the cap of the wine bottle, poured out three glasses, and handed one to me.

'I've only been inside the *Hare and Hounds* once,' he said, 'and that was once too often. I certainly shan't go tonight and miss this.'

So much for Angel's explanation for his nocturnal wanderings. I turned to give her a meaningful look, but she had suddenly become inexplicably interested in the contents of the salad bowl.

11

A Star is Born

'No, no you *must* remember to sit – how can you possibly use your seat to drive on forward if you keep rising to the trot? Try again. Take him across the diagonal, towards the corner, now sit down *hard*! Left rein, right leg behind the girth; sit and *push* – Oh, well done! I think you've mastered it! By the way,' Angel said, 'I won't be able to give you your lunge-lesson tomorrow morning, I'm seeing Hendor. I'm going to try and sell him our idea.'

Tearing my eyes from between the roan horse's ears, where I was supposedly training myself to look, I looked at Angel instead. Despite the blistering rays of a sun blazing fiercely out of a cloudless sky; heat that made the roan horse apathetic and caused the shirt to stick to my back, she still wore jeans and chaps. Her jodhpur boots were filmed with dust. But as a concession to the weather, the extravagant hair was twisted up and skewered on the top of her head with the pencil that should have been beside the tack room telephone.

'And ask him for supper?'

'Tomorrow night, I thought.'

'Good.' Sensing my inattention the roan dropped back into trot and from trot to walk. Although it was against the rules to allow the horse to make decisions on his own account, I let it happen, acknowledging by non-intervention that it was too hot for transitions.

Tomorrow looked as though it was going to be make or break day. Tomorrow we would know the outcome of the meeting between Hender and Anthony. Tomorrow I had made up my mind to ring Richard if he had not rung me before then. I was desperate to talk to Ziggy, to find out if my part in the television serial was still safe. If something had gone wrong the consequences would be too terrible to contemplate. My career would be over even before it had begun. I pushed it out of my mind. It was important to concentrate on my riding. There was not a lot of time left.

The roan horse with the white stockings stopped by the gate, hoping the lesson was over, longing if not for the cool of a stable, for the blessing of a shady tree. I closed my legs to his sides. Reluctantly, he walked on.

'Angel, how am I doing? There is such a lot to learn. I'm terrified I'm not going to be good enough.'

'You don't have to be all that good, not to start with, not to play a cripple,' she said.

'To play a *what*!' I stopped the roan horse. I stared at her. 'To play a WHAT?'

'To play a cripple.' Angel now looked horrified. 'Grace, you did *know*! They have *told* you she's crippled!'

'But I had no idea! Nobody has told me anything! A *cripple*? She can't be a cripple – how could she possibly ride?'

Angel looked at me in confusion. 'Look, I'm sorry, I shouldn't have said anything. Maybe she isn't so crippled, but from what I'd heard it was part of the story – you know, not being able to join in, do anything, until the horse came along.'

'But how do you know this much? Who told you?' The roan horse stretched his head, pulled the reins through my hands, rubbed his nose on the inside of his knee.

'I don't remember. It was just something somebody said, ages ago, before you came.' Angel was desperately evasive. 'You'll just have to forget I said it. After all, it might not be true.'

I pulled the roan's head up. It wasn't that I minded if

it was true. At least it would give me a part to get my teeth into, to prove that I could act. To prove to *myself* that I could act. It was just the way Angel had dropped it, like a bombshell, in the middle of the lesson. And why did she know so much, when I knew nothing? Well, I thought grimly, tomorrow I am going to find out a few things about the script, about the part, and about ATC. We resumed the lesson.

I rode the roan horse with the white stockings along the rails and tried to retain his attention. It was not easy because my mind was no longer on the lesson and the roan had had enough of transitions.

At the far end of the paddock, the woods were dark and cool and inviting. Standing at the edge, beyond a shimmer of heat haze, Anthony stood, watching. Did he know I was to play a cripple? Did Ziggy know? Did everyone know except me?

It was no good. It was impossible to concentrate. I stopped the roan horse. At practically the same moment Anthony appeared coming from the direction of the stables, leading the brown horse he was training to be a faller. I looked across at the woods. It was impossible for a person to be in two places at once. Now there was nobody watching from beyond the heat haze.

'We shall have to stop the lesson,' I said to Angel. 'I think the sun has got to my brain.'

'Get Angel. Tell her the mare's foaling.'

Anthony's terse command reached me as I was filling and weighing hay nets in the barn, speckled with seeds, doing my best not to sneeze. Dust from the hay swirled in the block of sunlight falling through the open doors.

I ran outside. 'She isn't here! She's gone to the village!' Actually, she had gone to see Hender, but it was not quite the moment to divulge that. Nor had it been the moment to ring Richard, his office had informed me that he was not there and was not expected back all day. I was already feeling frantic. Now there was this to contend with.

'Then it will have to be you, won't it.' Anthony strode off with unmerciful steps towards the foaling box.

'Oh, but I can't!' Yet I knew I should have to. Terrified, I ran after him, still stuck with wisps of hay, not knowing what I was supposed to be doing, thinking of towels and boiling water, forceps, swaddling clothes, all the usual impedimenta of a birth as practiced in the theatre, not knowing if any of it was applicable to horses.

In the foaling box, the mare was lying on her side with patches of sweat dark on her neck, her ribcage rising and falling with her heavy breathing. Her eyes were open and strained. Her nose wrinkled with distress and effort.

'Oh God,' I said, 'I can't help. I shall be useless.'

'Nonsense.' Anthony took my hand and pulled me inside. 'If everything goes normally, you won't have to do anything. We're only here just in case.'

I didn't want to be there just in case. I was frightened. The straw was wet and churned up. The mare gave a deep and gusting sigh.

'Let me wait outside,' I said. 'If anything goes wrong you can call me.' I knew if he did call me I would go out like a light.

'Calm down, Grace Darling. Keep quiet. You're supposed to be a calming influence on the mare. A comfort.'

I need some comfort myself. I knelt at the mare's head. With a hand that trembled I stroked the sweating neck.

'Steady girl,' I said. 'Everything's going to be fine.'

Anthony grinned. He moved towards her quarters. Towards her outflung tail. The mare went into a

91

convulsion that almost turned her eye sockets inside out.
I bit back a scream.

'The foal's coming,' Anthony said. 'Look.'

I couldn't bear to look, but somehow I looked anyway.
Two tiny hooves were emerging. Now I was petrified that
the foal would not get out, there didn't seem enough room.
But as the mare raised her upper hind leg slightly and
strained, lifting her head from the straw in the effort, a little
black crinkled nose appeared, and a face, lying along
impossibly long and slender forelegs, then a neck and a
body, clothed in a silver membrane, and finally, with a last,
gigantic effort which caused the mare to groan aloud, the
whole perfect foal slid out on to the straw.

Now I knew why people said birth was a miracle.

The foal, still mostly encased in his silver sack, struggled
in an exhausted fashion to free himself, striking out with
his tiny hooves. Anthony helped, pulling the tough
membrane away from him gently.

Now I was afraid that the mare didn't want her foal.

'She hasn't looked at him. She isn't taking any notice!'

'She will. She's just exhausted. They are both
exhausted.'

The foal pulled up his legs and rested his nose on the
straw. He did not look around at the amazing new world
he had suddenly been projected into. His eyes looked
blank, unfocused.

'Is the foal a filly or a colt?'

'He's a colt. A star is born.'

'Oh.' I had hoped for a filly. Now the mare lifted her
head and looked round at the colt. She looked at him, it
seemed, in curiosity, as if she wondered where he had come
from. She drew up her legs and stretched out her neck. She
gave him an experimental lick. The foal made a small
sound. Unexpectedly and with a great commotion the

mare struggled to her feet. Anthony and I instinctively moved away backwards to the side of the stable.

The mare stood and nuzzled the colt. After a while he made a feeble effort to get up but fell down immediately. He tried again on legs which wobbled furiously and collapsed once more. I wanted to rush forward to help, to hold him up, but I knew I must not interfere. I noticed that the mare seemed to be bleeding. I clutched at Anthony in dismay.

'It's all right, Grace Darling. It's the afterbirth. She has to get rid of it.'

This time I didn't look. I turned away, feeling squeamish. When I looked back the foal was up, balancing on its impossibly long, clumsy legs, reaching out its head, perilously unsteady, towards the mare's flank.

'Cross your fingers now,' Anthony whispered. 'This is the crucial part.'

I held my breath as the foal nuzzled the mare's flank. He didn't seem to be able to see what he was after, it was a blindly instinctive search, but bumping and swaying he finally encountered a bulging teat and fastened on to it as if to a lifeline.

Anthony let out a long sigh of relief. 'Thank the Lord for that. Now we can leave them in peace.'

'I can't bear the thought of him being a faller.' I looked at the foal, wet, tiny, his knees threatening to buckle under him at any moment and I didn't want him to grow up to be a stunt horse. I was afraid for him.

'He may not have to be. The brown horse is working well, and after all, Hender Copper has a pretty good faller.'

I could not believe I had heard it. I gaped at Anthony. Anthony kept his eyes on the foal. 'Yesterday evening Hender and I had quite a long talk on the telephone. I think we shall come to some sort of arrangement. I think we shall have to. It seems my hand is forced. If I am honest, I have known it for a long time,' he said.

'You don't mean ...?'

'I mean, Grace Darling, that somehow I seem to have got myself a partner. And Angel has not gone to the village at all, has she?'

'She's gone to ask Hender to supper! To sell him the idea of a partnership!'

Anthony smiled one of his thin smiles. 'How surprised she is going to be when she finds that not only have I already sold him the idea, but that he has also accepted *my* invitation to supper!'

It was all too much for me. Racked with emotion, limp like a washed-out rag after the birth of the colt, I now had to cope with Anthony's calm acceptance of a partnership with Hender, and the relief of knowing the foal would not have to be a faller. I leaned back against the wall. I felt frighteningly weak. Tears I did not know I had shed ran down my cheeks.

'I always imagined actresses had to be paid to cry.'

Anthony lifted my chin, lowered his head, and put his lips on to mine.

I had never expected he could be gentle. With a horse maybe, but not with a person, certainly not with an actress.

When I opened my eyes I would not have been surprised if my whole consistency had changed, melted into something quite different, like a chocolate bar left too long in the sun.

But everything was just the same.

Apart from the fact that Richard was standing in the open doorway, looking into the stable with eyes as cold as a glacier.

12
Amazing Grace

'Richard, I *promise* you! It just happened on the spur of the moment! It has never happened before and it will never happen again! There was nothing to it!'

'There seemed to be quite a lot to it. It looked entirely premeditated to me. Entirely. You have never kissed me like that,' Richard said in an icy voice.

'But that's absolute rubbish!'

'It wasn't as if I was unexpected. You knew I would arrive at any moment.'

'I didn't expect you at all!' Over the bonnet of the red Porsche 924 with the immaculate black pin-stripe upholstery I gaped at him. 'I had no idea you were coming this morning! You just turned up out of the blue! You *said* you would ring!'

'I did ring. I rang yesterday evening. I spoke to a girl who said you were busy – collecting sticks I believe she said, although I find *that* hard to swallow – but she did promise faithfully to deliver the message.'

Angel. It must have been Angel. I gritted my teeth. It *would* have been Angel! 'I *was* collecting sticks. The Aga had gone out. But I didn't get the message, Richard, *honestly*!'

'So I wasn't expected.'

'No.'

'I suppose that should make it easier, but somehow it doesn't.' He opened the car door.

I could not let him leave. 'Richard, *please* don't go! I swear to you that Anthony isn't in the least interested in me! You don't even have to take my word for it – go and ask him!'

With his hand on the door-handle, he looked at me in distaste. 'I would prefer not to.'

'I'm sure you would. I suppose it would dent your dignity.'

'My dignity is already irredeemably dented.' He got into the driving seat. It seemed that desperate measures would have to be employed in order to prevent his departure. I tried to open the passenger door. It was locked. I ran round to his side of the car just in time to catch the door before it slammed shut. I wrenched it open again. '*Richard*! *Please*! Don't GO! I *need* you! I have to get to *London*!'

Richard's hand froze on the ignition key. He looked at me in disbelief. 'I *beg* your pardon?'

Totally distraught, I poured it all out in a jumble; my anxiety about the non-appearance of the script, the unsuccessful attempts to contact Ziggy, my last telephone call to the Café Marengo, the disconnected signal, and the ensuing conversation with Directory Enquiries. How I was convinced that something had gone terribly wrong and my whole career might possibly be in ruins. How desperately I needed to get to Soho, and how he was the only person in the world who could help me.

Richard listened to all this with incredulous wonderment and at the end of it all his head dropped forward until it rested on the padded leather steering wheel with the Porsche insignia in the centre. I did not know if he was going to laugh or cry. Luckily he started to laugh.

'Grace, you are incredible! You never fail to amaze me! You tell me you want a cooling-off period, you ring me up to say you have changed your mind, I arrive to find you kissing another man, then you tell me it meant nothing and beg me not to leave – not because you are *sorry*, not even because of my charm and good looks – but because you want me to drive you to London!'

Put like that it did not show me in a very good light, but what could I say? What else could I do? 'Richard, *will* you take me?'

He leaned back in the pin-stripe seat and sighed. 'I don't suppose you thought to ring the television company when your script failed to arrive?'

'I thought about it, but I had no idea who to ask for. Most of the producers and directors who make television programmes are freelance anyway. Only Ziggy knows who we are dealing with because he does all the negotiating, it's his job to chase them, not mine.'

'And you say the Café Marengo has gone Ex-Directory?'

'According to Directory Enquiries, and I've checked twice.'

'I can't believe it.'

'Neither can I.'

In an agony of suspense, I knelt by the car and looked at him imploringly. '*Please* Richard.'

'Grace,' he said eventually in a resigned voice, 'if I am to drive you to London, I think you had better run and get changed. You will look a little bizarre, even in Soho.'

'Then you'll take me!' I would have hugged him, but an outstretched hand held me off lest I soil the immaculate elegance of his cream cotton trousers, his black and cream striped *Dunhill* jersey – I was, after all, somewhat dirty and dishevelled, stuck with straw and stained with manure, my hair decorated with hayseeds. 'Richard, you are a brick! I won't be ten seconds!'

'I have always wanted to be a brick,' he said in a humourless tone as I raced off towards the farmhouse.

13

This Bright, New Talent ...

Something had happened at the Café Marengo.

As the car nudged its way along the narrow street between the strip clubs with a tout in every neon-lit doorway; past the dubious magazine shops, the non-stop film shows, the delicatessens whose windows were heaped with bread and freshly made pasta; skirting groups of tourists and noisy gangs of provincial youths, emboldened by numbers, who individually would have been too embarrassed to walk through Soho, we could see a crowd outside, their noses pressed to the window.

As usual, there was not a parking space to be had. Richard stopped amidst the bustle, waving off a swarthy woman who pushed a sprig of lucky white heather under his nose. 'I shall have to drop you here and put the car in the multi-storey car park. I'll come to you as quickly as I can.'

I ran along the pavement, dodging dawdling couples and determined ladies with shopping baskets heading for the fruit and vegetable market off Brewer Street. I had no idea what I was going to find, but I had a nasty feeling it was not going to be to my advantage.

A queue of people waited to enter the Café Marengo. I had no time to wait. I pushed my way past them, ignoring their protests. Inside, every seat was taken. The corner booth from which Ziggy had conducted his business was now occupied by an American family forking up pasta and gulping milk shakes. There was a new face behind the counter.

I squeezed myself into a space between people sitting

on bar stools. 'Please, where can I find Mr Vincinelli?' I was terribly afraid the new face would tell me he had no idea, that the Café Marengo was Under New Management.

But the new face looked up from the black cherry cheesecake he was serving and gestured towards the coffee machine at the end of the counter. Behind it, I found Mr Vincinelli looking dangerously overwrought, holding a jug of milk under the steam spout, waiting for the bubbles to rise with a fevered impatience.

I poked my head through the chrome. 'Mr Vincinelli! It's me, Grace Darling! I'm looking for Ziggy! What's happened? Where have all these people come from? Why are they here?'

Mr Vincinelli looked at me in astonishment. 'You mean you do not see the newspapers!' He shot milky froth on to several waiting cups of coffee and rushed them to the counter. Over the clatter of cups and saucers in preparation for the next batch he said in a passionate voice, 'You want to know what has happened, Miss Grace Darling? I tell you what has happened! What has happened is that my business is overflown and I am become a nervous wreckage, that is what has happened!' With one hand he poured coffee into the cups and with the other he produced a tabloid newspaper which he thrust at my face. 'Here, I show you this! Then perhaps you understand better! You see the front page? Now you believe me when I tell you it is all the fault of Mr Stanislavski and the girl with the big voice who last time she was here frighten away all my customers! Now I have too many customers!' Mr Vincinelli thrust another jug of milk under the steam spout. Over the hissing and gurgling noise he said emotionally, 'Before this happen, Miss Grace Darling, if you ask me do I want more customers, I tell you yes, because my business it is not so good, but now I have too much, is too many for me, when you see Mr Stanislavski you tell him that ...'

I looked at the front page of the tabloid. The headlines leapt out. UNKNOWN GIRL PICKED TO STAR IN WEST END MUSICAL. *Emma Hall wows Lloyd-Webber and snatches the part from established stars. 'This bright, new talent with her astonishing voice is set for instant fame' says our Special Theatrical Correspondent.* The photograph under the headlines was of a face I recognized only too well. Emma Hall's face. A face with large, clear eyes and a determined expression, framed with thick blonde hair sliced to the level of her ear lobes.

'Because of this newspaper, all day long I have the acting and singing girls asking for Mr Stanislavski! Because of this newspaper I have all these new customers – my old customers they take one look and they run! I tell you, Miss Grace Darling, it is too much for me! Even when I sleep I make the coffee, I serve the pasta, and when I wake up it is time to start again! Every day I have the people from the newspapers and they ask me questions. How do you like the new business, they ask me, How do you like to be famous? How do you feel? Well, I tell you how I feel,' Mr Vincinelli said in a furious voice. 'I feel tired! That's how I feel!'

I could not take my eyes away from the newspaper. Emma Hall had auditioned for Ziggy in the Café Marengo only three months ago. I had been here at the time. To Emma Hall Ziggy had said, 'Go away. Go get a day job in a nice shop. Get singing lessons four nights a week. On the other three nights get dancing lessons. In your lunch hours get acting lessons.' I had watched as the clear blue eyes had flooded with disappointment. 'Oh rats,' Emma Hall had said. 'Am I that bad?' To which Ziggy had replied 'You're not as good as you got to be, and that's a fact.'

Mr Vincinelli clattered out another batch of cups and saucers. He stuck another jug of milk under the steam spout. 'I like to see Mr Stanislavski for myself at this moment,' he said explosively. 'I like to show him what he has done to my business, to the Café Marengo! You know what he say to me? I have to split, Vincinelli, he say to me; the Café Marengo it is too noisy for me, it is too crowded, it is affecting my business! I ask you! Is that his fault or mine?' He topped the coffee and raced off along the counter.

Further down the page there was a smaller photograph of Emma Hall standing outside the Café Marengo. In the doorway stood Mr Vincinelli in his apron, looking harassed. *'My agent works from a Soho café,' says the girl who is set to be the toast of London's West End. 'At first, even he refused me. But I wouldn't give up. I was determined to succeed. Chance had nothing to do with it. Luck had nothing to do with it. It was hard work and perseverance that got me the break I needed.'*

Mr Vincinelli returned, throwing out more saucers, cups, spoons, pouring more coffee, steaming more milk. 'Mr Stanislavski he say to me: Vincinelli, this publicity forces me to go legit. I have to get licensed. I have to get an office! I would like to say this to Mr Stanislavski! Look what this publicity has done to me, to the Café Marengo!'

I should have been pleased for Emma Hall. I should have been delighted for her sake. But the headlines dug into my heart like a knife. Because I had wanted to be Ziggy's biggest success. As a reward for all his encouragement, his advice, his faith, I had wanted it to be Grace Darling who made his name. These headlines should have been mine.

'Mr Vincinelli, where *is* Ziggy? Where can I find him?'

Mr Vincinelli leaned backwards away from the

machine and grabbed a business card from a shelf. He pushed it through the gap. 'You go and see Mr Stanislavski now, Miss Grace Darling, and you give him a message from Mr Vincinelli! You tell him I need more staffings, I need more tables, I need bigger café, but most of all I need to sleep!'

'I will. I promise.'

Over the counter someone said to the new face, 'Which is the agent's booth? Is he here today?' I ran out into the street and collided with Richard. He looked at the card and hailed a cruising taxi.

The address was just a few streets away. On the pavement a young man was screwing a brass plate below all the other brass plates on one side of the doorway. Z. STANISLAVSKI. STARLIGHT PROMOTIONS, it said, 5TH FLOOR.

There was no lift. I raced up five flights leaving Richard to follow at his own pace. On the fifth floor I burst through a door and was confronted by a girl sitting at a desk with a typewriter, two telephones and a goose-foot plant.

'Can I help you?' she said. 'Do you have an appointment?'

It was a far cry from the corner booth in the Café Marengo.

'I don't need an appointment,' I gasped. 'I'm Grace Darling. I need to see Ziggy. It's urgent.'

'Grace Darling?' She frowned slightly. 'Should I know the name? Mr Stanislavski isn't actually here at the moment. I don't expect him back until four.'

'Four?' I looked at my watch. It was half past two.

Richard now appeared through the doors. 'Grace, I can't wait until four. It's impossible. I have to be back in Wallingford by seven for the company dinner. I can't miss it. I have to make a speech.'

Nor could I wait. I had a celebration dinner to cook.

I flopped into a chair next to the goose-foot plant and poured out all my troubles to the receptionist. She was sympathetic but there was not a lot she could do. She said I should go back to Moat Farm and telephone from there at five o'clock. By that time she would have explained the situation to Ziggy, but that she was sure I was over-reacting. Scripts were often late, she said, writers seemed unable to keep to any kind of time schedule. She was sure nothing had gone wrong.

Speeding back down the motorway, I sank back into my seat, drained and exhausted. Had I over-reacted? Perhaps I had, but at least I now knew why it was the Café Marengo had gone Ex-Directory. And I knew where to find Ziggy, and that was the important thing.

'I'm really terribly grateful to you for doing this,' I told Richard. 'Given the situation, most people would have refused.'

'I know.'

'Most people would have driven away and left me to rot.'

'I almost did.'

'I do appreciate it, Richard, honestly.'

'So you should.'

'I had no idea it was the company dinner tonight.'

No reply. Richard stared ahead.

'Last year, you invited me to go with you.'

'Last year and the year before that,' he reminded me.

'But not this year.'

'No.'

'Why not?'

'Last year you were in London, looking for work. The year before you were at Drama School. This year you are at Moat Farm.'

'But you could have asked.'

'To give you the pleasure of refusing?'

'I might not have refused.'

'With a cast iron excuse like Moat Farm, I rather think you would have.'

'I suppose so.' I was rather peeved though, not to have been asked. 'So you're going alone.'

'Did I say that?'

'Not exactly. You mean you're not going alone?'

'I'm not going alone,' Richard confirmed.

'Then who ...?'

'I'm taking Marcia Cunningham.'

I might have known it. Marcia Cunningham was Richard's ever-steady standby. Marcia Cunningham with her lavish statistics, her pouting lips and her luxuriant mass of auburn hair. I loathed Marcia Cunningham. I sat up in my seat, outraged. 'After all the fuss you made today about an innocent kiss, now you tell me you're taking Marcia Cunningham to the company dinner tonight! Richard, how *could* you?'

Richard removed his eyes from the road long enough to give me a coolly amused glance.

'I suppose you'll kiss Marcia Cunningham!'

'I expect I shall do rather more than that.'

I froze. All the way back to Moat Farm I sat stiffly in my seat and maintained a stony silence. Richard, having turned the tables in his habitual manner, drove with infuriating composure. When we arrived he opened the car door for me with polite attention, pecked my frozen cheek and drove away down the bumpy drive towards Wallingford, towards the company dinner, towards Marcia Cunningham. Had I a gun I would have put a bullet through every tyre.

The farmhouse kitchen was empty. So was the office. There was a note beside the telephone written on a piece of crumpled paper retrieved from the wastepaper basket.

RING DIRECTOR ABOUT FLYING HORSE SEQUENCE – CONVEYOR BELT?

As I dialled Ziggy's number I turned over the crumpled paper in a furious and distracted manner. It was a page of script for *The Hooves of the Horses*.

14
Everything Has Its Price

I flew out of the farmhouse and down the nettle path like a madwoman. Past the muckheap I pounded, past the open doors of the barn, into the stable yard, red hot with fury, looking for somebody, anybody.

I found Angel. She came out of The Raven's stable with his day rug over her arm. 'Oh good,' she said, 'you're back. I was just beginning to wonder about supper.'

'You can forget supper!' I shouted.

She looked at me in astonishment. I thrust the crumpled paper at her. 'I want an explanation for THIS!'

Angel looked at the paper. '*Ring Director re flying horse sequence – conveyor belt*? It's not so difficult really. We have to teach the horse to canter on a conveyor belt because then the action can be filmed in a studio against a plain blue background, after that the sky is shot separately ...'

I thought she was being deliberately obtuse. 'Not *that*! Look at the other *side*!'

She turned over the paper. There was no mistaking where the page was from because the title of the serial was on the top in bold type. 'Oh dear,' Angel said. 'Now I suppose you will have to know everything.' She paled.

'I think I can guess most of it! Obviously my script *did* arrive, and for reasons best known to ourselves, *you* appropriated it!'

'It wasn't like that at all.' Angel looked apprehensive. She folded up the rug and put it on the ground. 'I think you had better come with me.'

'No wonder you always got to the postbox first! No

wonder you didn't want me to call at the Post Office! You knew it was here all the *time*!'

'That wasn't the reason. You are wrong,' Angel said.

I followed her past the open doors of the barn, past the muckheap.

'No wonder you knew I was playing a *cripple*!'

Angel gave me a nervous look. She began to run.

I ran after her. 'And whilst you are explaining why you stole my script, you can also explain why you failed to tell me that Richard was coming today!'

Angel speeded up. She raced along the nettle path. 'I forgot! There was a message and I was going to write it down, but I couldn't find the pencil!'

I didn't believe it. 'That isn't true! It was all part of some crazy plan, Angel! *Admit* it!'

'I won't! It wasn't! I've *told* you, I just forgot to pass on the message! You told me he was ugly and boring! You said you wished he would leave you alone! It didn't seem all that important!' Angel cried.

She sped across the wilderness, towards the wood. I had no idea if she was taking me somewhere, or if she was just trying to run away. I tried to grab the back of her shirt. She looked back at me, terrified.

'Where is my script!' I yelled at her. 'What have you done with it!' I made a wild lunge towards her streaming hair. She screamed.

Along the hoof-flattened path we raced. Into the wood. Into the darkness. Up to the pantomime cottage. In through the door.

Once inside Angel threw open another door leading into the only habitable room, the one where the glass was still intact. Leaning against the wall was Anthony. Sitting at a table behind a forest of whisky bottles and a typewriter was somebody who, viewed through a heat-haze and at a distance, could also have been Anthony, but was actually Tom Sylvester.

Angel collapsed against the door-frame. Her breath came out in sobs. 'I had to bring her,' she panted. 'I thought she was going to murder me.'

I should have realized they were brothers, they were so alike, and of course Angel had not been beating me to the post to appropriate my script, but to prevent me from seeing letters addressed to Anthony Sylvester. That would have given the game away. And Tom had been adamant that I should not know he was working so close, he knew I would have pestered him for bits of the script, for the story, for details of the character I was to play. And when I had calmed down enough to consider it, I had to admit that he was right.

There were six at the celebration dinner. Ziggy drove from London to be there. Many toasts were drunk to the new partnership, to the engagement of Angel and Hender, to the completed script, to my success in the part, to Ziggy's new premises, to the birth of the colt, even to Emma Hall's West End début.

But later on, I slipped away on the pretext of checking the mare and foal and wandered round the stable yard. I stood and looked over the stable door at the mare who had been the best faller in the business as she lay serenely in the straw with her sleeping son. The roan with the long white stockings who was loose because he liked to be loose came to stand beside me.

I had only been at Moat farm for three weeks but it seemed like years. Horses were part of my life now. And ahead was the making of the series and whatever adventures that may bring. One thing was certain, as an actress, I would either be a success or a failure at the end of it.

But I was to have my chance and that was all I had wanted. And if somewhere in Wallingford, Richard was heavily involved with Marcia Cunningham, I supposed that everything had its price.

Have you seen
NANCY DREW
lately?

Nancy Drew has become a girl of the 80s! There is hardly a girl from seven to seventeen who doesn't know her name.

Now you can continue to enjoy Nancy Drew in a new series, written for older readers – THE NANCY DREW FILES. Each book has more romance, fashion, mystery and adventure.

In THE NANCY DREW FILES, Nancy pursues one thrilling adventure after another. With her boundless energy and intelligence, Nancy finds herself enrolling at a crime-ridden high school, attending rock concerts and locating the missing star, skiing in Vermont with friends Bess and George and faithful boyfriend Ned, and temping at a teenage magazine based in wildly exciting New York.

COMING IN SPRING 1988

The Nancy Drew Files

No. 1 Secrets Can Kill
No. 2 Deadly Intent
No. 3 Murder on Ice
No. 4 Smile and Say Murder

ARMADA

Forthcoming teenage fiction
published in Armada

ARMADA

STEVIE DAY SUPERSLEUTH
(that's me!)

I'm on my way to being the first female Commissioner of the Metropolitan Police. It's true I have a few personal problems: for a start I'm small and skinny and people are always mistaking me for a boy. I'm 14 – though you wouldn't think so – and my younger sister, Carla, not only looks older than me but she's much prettier too. Not that that really matters. You see, she doesn't have my brains.

If you want to see my razor-sharp mind in action or have proof of my brilliant powers of deduction then read about my triumphant successes in:

STEVIE DAY: Supersleuth
STEVIE DAY: Lonely Hearts
STEVIE DAY: Rat Race